TWO AGAINST THE STARS

VERONICA SCOTT

To my daughters, Valerie and Elizabeth; my brother, David and my best friend, Daniel, for all their encouragement and support! And to Pauline – hugs!

ACKNOWLEDGMENTS

Julie C and The E-book Formatting Fairies!

CHAPTER ONE

Carialle rubbed her right wrist where the cuff was chafing the skin and curled tighter against the headboard, watching Dobkin as he frantically worked the vidcoms, in between taking hits of feelgood.

Her Amarotu Combine handler threw his personal AI against the wall and cursed in three languages. "Where the seven hells is everyone?" Rising from the desk chair, he paced around the cheap hotel room as he ran one hand through his greasy hair. "It's like they all disappeared or fell into a black hole."

She noted with interest how unsteady his gait was and the way his words were beginning to slur. Today might be her chance to escape. Certainly this job hadn't gone like any of their others, beginning with the moment she first roused from cryo sleep imprisonment, nauseous and dizzy, to find herself in a cargo warehouse alone with Dobkin. No local contact had met him, which was unheard of. Their team of two came in to do a task and depart the planet just as rapidly, not to flounder on their own. Use of Carialle's time and powers cost the customers a fortune so a local liaison was required to meet them and expedite the arrangements.

At the warehouse, Dobkin had gotten her out of the concealed cryo chamber, released her shackles, seeming glad of her company for once. He was plainly rattled if he was being nice to her. He sealed the cargo crate where she'd been concealed with a thump revealing the state of his emotions. For an hour he'd prowled the private cargo office the Combine maintained, making fruitless calls, before abruptly deciding to rent a ground car, find a cheap hotel and regroup. Now here she and her handler sat, in a room smelling of harsh disinfectants and stale smoke, hours later and still no wiser.

Carialle looked with distaste at the serving of greasy food he'd given her after fastening her handcuff to the bed. Her stomach roiled after a few bites. With her free hand she pushed the now-congealed offering further away.

Dobkin pulled a bottle of cheap whiskey from his pack and took a hefty swig just as the AI pinged for an incoming call. Stumbling, he retrieved the unit and accepted the comlink. "At last. Edmorad, where have you been? Why didn't anyone meet me at the spaceport? Time is money where these services are involved."

"It's a mess, man. No one knows exactly what's going on. Where the seven hells have *you* been, not to have heard the news?" The voice on the other end of the call was nearly hysterical and so loud Carialle heard the words easily.

"The Combine booked us on a slow freighter so I've been in transit until today." Shaking his head, Dobkin clenched his fingers tighter on the AI unit. "Never mind my itinerary, what's happened?"

"Well for starters your base on Devir Six was blown up by the SCIA. Must have been right after you left. Then the rumor is the cops hit the big overlords' secret meeting, wherever *they* were. Not secret enough obviously. Everyone left has gone to ground, securely under cover. I suggest you do the same. No one's in charge right now and the situation is way out of control, every sentient for himself. Find a safe den and stay there. Good luck." With a click the link closed and no one answered when Dobkin tried to call back.

He sank onto the desk chair, swigging the alcoholic beverage straight from the container absent mindedly.

Carialle tried to piece together the fragments of information, based on her limited knowledge of the Sectors. If the base on Devir Six was gone, taken off the board by the Sectors Criminal Investigation Agency, then the rest of her people were gone as well. *No one left to be a hostage for my good behavior.* She'd had no close friends there, no loved ones, but sorrow for those who'd died choked her breathing and brought tears to her eyes. Impatiently she swiped the moisture away with her free hand. She had to concentrate on Dobkin, because her life depended on his whim.

He was eyeing her now. "Well, this is a shitstorm but at least I'm left with an ace." He strolled to the bed, staggering as he walked. Fingering her hair while she shrank against the pillows, he said, "You're a high value asset in anyone's game and now you're all mine. I just may come out of this on top. This could be Lan Dobkin's lucky day. Go freelance, set my own terms." Relishing the visions he was contemplating, he took another drink.

Wandering to the desk again, Dobkin selected a handful of colorful feelgood tabs from his stash and washed them down with a generous amount of the whiskey.

For the thousandth time, Carialle wished her power worked on Dobkin. As she understood matters, her ability affected 95% of humans and humanoids, but in certain rare sentients there was a genetic quirk shielding them from her use of empathy. The Combine had combed their ranks for men and women with the trait, to become the handlers for their new slaves.

Dobkin took another drink and set the bottle precariously close to the edge of the desk. Rising, he fumbled with the fastening of his trousers. "Gotta answer nature's call," he said, walking a crooked line to the small bathroom, bumping into the desk and the bureau as he proceeded.

The light came on in the tiny space and a moment later, Carialle heard a thud and a groan. "Dobkin?"

No answer.

She waited, counting to one hundred, and called his name a second time. No response, not even a groan.

Heart pounding, she turned to the old fashioned headboard, which featured elaborate knobs at the top of each post, including the one her wrist was chained to. She knew Dobkin hadn't noticed since he'd been well on the way to literally falling down drunk, but the ornate knobs were threaded onto the posts. Now she spun the orb atop the post holding her cuff until the decorative piece fell to the floor with a clunk. Raising her arm to bring the anchor cuff up and over the top of the post, she slid off the bed. Freezing in place like a terrified woods creature, holding her breath, she gazed in the direction of the bathroom. *It's now or never.* Grabbing the abandoned bottle to use as a weapon, she crept toward the half open door, only to stop short of the threshold with a gasp.

Her handler lay sprawled on the cheap imitation tile floor, a pool of blood spreading from the back of his head. He'd evidently fallen or passed out from the drugs he'd done, striking his head on the commode as he toppled. His sporadic breathing was labored and halted on a harsh exhale even as she stared at him. His head lolled to the side and his entire body went limp.

Her heightened senses confirmed Dobkin's lifeforce had fled.

The handler's death left her numb. He'd never assaulted her, nor beaten her, as some of the other handlers did with their charges, but he'd been casually cruel since they met. He clearly didn't see her as a person in her own right. Indeed, not as anything but a tool to use for the Combine's profit and his own advancement.

"I'm not going to be used for anyone else's purposes ever again," she said

Setting the bottle aside, Carialle swallowed hard and forced herself to go through his pockets, snagging the AI control for her deadly explosive-laden necklace, the key to the handcuffs and his ID and credit tag. Her hands were shaking so hard it took her three tries to release the shackle around her wrist but then she pushed the button on the AI to unclasp the deadly golden necklace – another incentive for good behavior the Combine forced their empathic slaves to wear. Weeping, she caught the gaudy pendant as it fell away from her neck.

"Four years and how many deaths, you bastards?" She took a deep breath to quell her rising hysteria. *No time to waste.* Struck by a grimly amusing idea, she locked the explosive device around Dobkin's neck. It wasn't real gold anyway and the gems were also fake, so she couldn't hope to sell it for any credits. Let whoever came to investigate figure out the mystery.

Carialle unfastened a gaudy, retro timepiece from his wrist and sidled away. It took her a few moments in the bedroom to dump out the contents of his small pack, snatching whatever might be useful and leaving the rest on the bed. She contemplated the small hand weapon for a long moment. She'd no idea how to use it but the allure of possessing a means of defending herself against those immune to her power was impossible to resist. Grabbing the shiny mini blaster, she hid it at the bottom of the pack and sealed the seams.

She straightened her spine, took a deep breath and checked the mirror to be sure there was no blood on her drab gray tunic, leggings or shoes. She hastened to the door and stepped into the hall, closing the portal behind her, keying the advisory to Do Not Disturb.

Her emotions were running on overdrive, with adrenaline, disbelief and a wild joy mixing to give her the shakes. She forced herself to walk slowly through the corridor to the gravlift and once in the lobby to duck out a side door and head away from the hotel at a measured pace. She wanted to run as fast as she could but the key to a successful escape was appearing as if she belonged on this street, as if everything was normal. Although of course there were no other sentients of her own race in the throngs of pedestrians, she observed many aliens mixed with the Terran-descent humans in the crowd. No one would give her a second glance. She wouldn't stand out too much, although her hair was distinctive in its fernlike qualities. *Nothing I can do— buy a scarf maybe.* She stopped at a credit machine and withdrew as much as she could from Dobkin's account, thanking her good fortune people on this planet apparently still dealt with actual money. She'd watched him perform this transaction enough times to know how he accessed his resources. Regretfully she tossed his credit tag into the nearest waste disposal bin, where it would be vaporized with all the other trash. The risk of being tracked was too high to use it again.

Walking onward, she found a mass transit stop and boarded the first vehicle to arrive. She didn't care where it took her as long as she was further away from where she'd last been seen with the Combine handler.

Carialle rode the line all day, well into the afternoon, working her way into seedier and more rundown portions of the city. Fortunately the planet was a Sector

Hub, so there was a diverse mix of humans and humanoids throughout the city, which made her appearance unremarkable. True, there were no others exactly like her—how could there be, when her home planet lay far away, outside the Sectors in enemy territory? But neither did she stand out, even this far away from the spaceport. She made one stop, to sell Dobkin's wrist chrono for a few credits at a pawn shop, to add to her stockpile, after which she took another transit vehicle going in the opposite direction.

Eventually she got off the transit line and walked deeper into the uninviting area she'd chosen. No stranger to the poor, hardscrabble side of life, she wasn't afraid to venture into the slums. She'd find her way somehow and her power to influence others would protect her. Pausing to watch the activity at a line of street vendors, she worked out what the proper amount of credits must be and then strolled over to a cart whose offerings smelled delicious. Taking the plate of gravy-covered meat, noodles and crisp vegetables, plus a drink, she sat on a bench in the small park nearby, among crowds of other people eating their early dinner or late lunch. The trees and flowers were sparse, tired-looking, but she absorbed energy anyway. Thank Thuun this planet was blessed with bountiful plant life.

After finishing her meal, surprised at how healthy her appetite was after the traumatic events of the day, she wandered through the area, which boasted small shops with the proprietors' living quarters above. The neighborhood was crowded and lively with street musicians playing for credits. Carialle kept her eyes open for any signs of Combine activity but detected none. Oh, there were scammers and pickpockets, but when she touched them lightly with her highly attuned senses, the petty crooks had no thought of the Combine.

It doesn't mean they wouldn't sell me out in a heartbeat, but at least for now they pose no threat.

Reassured she'd made a good choice, she strolled further, observing the mix of older, poorly maintained buildings and the newer, refurbished places. Obviously a neighborhood in transition but not too far into becoming more prosperous territory yet. She encountered no police or authorities of any kind, which for her was just as reassuring as not seeing Combine enforcers. Who could predict how the mysterious authorities would view what she'd done as a Combine tool? And she'd probably be suspected of killing Dobkin, which was another huge problem.

High in the azure sky, the glint of an ascending spacecraft drew her attention for a moment. Averting her gaze, she blinked away tears. This planet was going to be her home for the rest of her life. Being without official papers locked her onto the surface of this world. She doubted she'd ever be able to afford fake ID good enough to board a spaceship openly. *And where would I go anyway?*

Deciding her first priority was a place to live, she was delighted to see a rooms-for-rent sign on a gray building a few blocks to the south of the marketplace square. She keyed the signal button on the gate.

"Yes?" The voice was querulous.

"I'd like to ask about renting a room."

"First week's rent in advance, cash money only, no credit."

Carialle smiled. *Does the woman think I was born yesterday?* "I need to see the room first."

"Fair enough. I'll be right down."

Carialle stepped into a patch of shade and waited. Eventually the old fashioned portal creaked open and she blinked at the elderly figure who peered out at her. Short, with white hair in intricate braids, the woman wore floating multicolor robes that reminded Carialle of how her visualization of the colors of other people's emotions appeared in her mind's eye. Belatedly she scanned the woman even as they shook hands and introduced themselves. She applied influence to make Mrs. Galaganos want to help her.

"I've recently arrived in the area and I need a place to stay," she said.

"We have a lot of turnover in the building, doesn't bother me as long as the rent's paid." The owner shrugged. "No refunds if a tenant leaves without adequate notice. City with a big spaceport like ours has, people are always coming and going. Not my business. Come inside and let me show you the apartment," the landlady said, drawing Carialle across the threshold.

She stopped, transfixed by the lush garden growing in the apartment building's hidden courtyard. Riotous blooms and vines were everywhere, accented by small trees, with a large shade tree in the center. A fountain burbled off to the left, supplying water to a fish pond beside it. Carialle felt her soul replenishing itself in the presence of so much carefully nurtured nature. The park had been pleasant but underwhelming. This was a true oasis.

Obviously pleased by her reaction, Mrs. Galaganos was grinning. "I like to garden."

"So I see. I could help, if I lived here." Drawn by the scent she went to the nearest flowering bush and bent to inhale a delicious whiff of deep perfume. "I'm quite good with plants."

"Point in your favor. The apartment is over this way." The elderly woman led her through the garden to a gaily painted door, which she keyed open, before preceding Carialle into the small unit. "Not much—a bedroom, bathroom, kitchenette and sitting area."

The space was clean and neat, the furniture battered but sturdy, and Carialle was astonished how much she wanted to call it her own, at least for a while. The cell on Devir 6 was a featureless cubicle with no window and a slab to sleep on. "How much?"

The landlady mentioned a number and added a security deposit whose size had Carialle swallowing hard. Her backpack contained enough credits for one month's lodging, with a bit left over for food. But to walk away from this place and the garden outside was impossible. "I'll take it."

"Good. Come upstairs to my place and we'll sign the lease."

"I'm not sure how long I'll be in the area. Can I stay month to month? No lease?" Carialle made her tone casual. "The less paperwork the better, right? Keep life simple."

Eyeing her up and down, the woman took a long time to nod her agreement. Carialle added to the pressure she was placing on Galaganos's innate desire to be helpful and to nurture others, and suppressed the landlady's natural curiosity as much as she dared. Oblivious to the emotional manipulation, the woman fell in with Carialle's desire for a temporary home. "All right, credits in advance, like I said."

Carialle set her pack on the sidewalk and retrieved the funds, counting out the agreed upon amount and restoring the pitiful remainder to safety. *Good thing I sold Dobkin's chrono.*

Moving faster than her wizened appearance suggested would be possible, Mrs. Galaganos scooped the credits into a pocket on her voluminous dress and hesitated. "Will you need a job by any chance?"

"Yes, actually, now that you ask, I do, but I don't have any papers."

"Few in this area are documented." Mrs. Galaganos chuckled as she pulled a cookie from another pocket and nibbled on the frosted edge. "Part of the appeal of this section of town, live and let live. Stay out of trouble, no one'll give you a hassle." She waggled a finger at Carialle. "No bringing anyone into my building, mind you. I run a clean establishment. I don't rent by the hour, if you follow me."

"Of course not." Carialle was nonplussed at the suggestion. "I hoped maybe one of the street vendors might need help cooking, or a local restaurant might need dishwashing perhaps. They didn't seem like places owning expensive servo robots. Do you have any suggestions?"

The elderly woman patted her hand. "If you aren't afraid of hard work, no one cares about the formalities. The Sector authorities have bigger fish to fry than whoever wanders into this slum. I know a place that's constantly looking for help. One of my friends told me a few days ago she'd lost a few employees. High attrition rate, not everyone can take working in the environment."

"What kind of place is this?" Carialle was prepared to accept pretty much anything in her current dire straits.

"It's a clinic and residential medical facility, handles pretty sick patients. Job's not much, primarily cleaning, but they pay a fair wage. The environment can get depressing. Stressful." She brushed crumbs from her skirt. "Or so the girls in apartment 6d have told me. Both of them work there and I've had a few other tenants get jobs as orderlies or cooks."

"I've done cleaning before." Carialle shoved away her memories of all the years she'd cleaned the nooks and crannies of the temple on Tulavarra.

"Go out the gate and turn left, walk about four blocks and find the Milning Rehab Clinic, ask for Mrs. Trang. You can tell them I sent you. Actually it's the manager I know best, Gretta, but Mrs. Trang likes to do her own hiring." Mrs. Galaganos sniffed. "She's on the cold, unpleasant side, spurned my friendly offer to help with an open house for the neighborhood when the clinic first opened. But Gretta says the clinic is well run." The landlady checked her own chrono. "You could go today, if you hurried."

"I might." The landlady was so pushy, Carialle speculated for a moment whether she got a commission from sending people to apply for the less than desirable jobs. She wanted to be alone, to relax and glory in her freedom for the first time in over four years, but the necessity to have an income drove her to leave the tiny apartment with her new landlady, and to head for the clinic. Going tomorrow when someone more enterprising might have already beaten her to the job wasn't a lost opportunity she could risk.

A relatively short walk away, the clinic was a neat building, blue with darker blue trim, surrounded by ruthlessly trimmed, thorny bushes. Wishing she was in a more presentable state, Carialle entered the lobby, impressed by how clean and organized it was. "I'm here about a job," she told the receptionist. "Mrs. Galaganos sent me. I'm supposed to ask for Mrs. Trang."

The woman frowned. "The owner isn't here today, but I think we do need a new person on the night cleaning crew. Sit over there and wait a minute—I'll get the manager."

Carialle took the indicated chair and a few moments later a harassed woman emerged from the hall on the right. Using her power to influence the newcomer to want to help her, Carialle stood, adding pressure to react positively and be impressed by her attitude. She subtly eased the woman's internal stress over her own problems to make room for cheerful acceptance of Carialle.

Hands on her hips, the manager surveyed her from head to toe. She didn't offer to shake hands or invite Carialle to go to a more private location, much less to fill out paperwork. The interview, such as it was, was plainly to be conducted in the middle of the bustling lobby, with workers and patients' family members brushing past. "I'm Gretta Nestrum. You have experience?"

"In cleaning, not nursing or anything taking care of patients." She figured honesty was her best approach here. "Mrs. Galaganos suggested I—"

Gretta unbent a little, a small smile on her face. "Granny Galaganos sends us people from time to time. I think she wants to be sure her tenants can pay their rent—she has no idea what skills I need. But she means well enough." Gretta cleared her throat. "I have orderlies and aides to take care of the patients but you could be in luck—one of my janitors quit yesterday. Can you start tonight? Now?" Gretta eyed her again, taking in the plain gray tunic and pants.

"Of course, if you need help." Carialle made her voice humble and eager.

"We pay minimum wage, credits in the hand weekly. You handle your own taxes. We don't do any paperwork." Gretta raised one elegantly shaped blue eyebrow and tilted her head, clearly waiting to see if Carialle had any issue with the legalities.

The less of a trail I leave, the better. "Who needs the extra hassle?" she said.

"I supply the uniforms. You'll have to buy the right shoes tomorrow— we'll tell you where and you get a discount since you work here. You'll be on probation for a week, then if you do a good job, keep your nose clean, I'll make you a regular, give you a set shift of hours. Of course you'll have to have an interview with the owner, Mrs. Trang, but she isn't here today. We can at least get you working and solve part of my problem in the meantime, till she approves you. Follow me." Gretta led the way past the reception desk and along a gleaming corridor, into an employee dressing room, with lockers. Taking a tunic and leggings from a rack of similar garments, she handed the clothing to Carialle. "Go ahead and change and I'll send Dak Peters to fetch you. Shadow him for tonight, do whatever he wants done. Our cleaning robos are old but well maintained and we do require hand cleaning of specific areas, for the benefit of the patients. You may have to deal with hazardous biological messes from time to time, since many of our patients are quite critically ill but I assume you can handle the tasks."

"Biological messes?"

"Blood, vomit, other substances. Does the idea bother you?" Eyes narrowed, head thrust forward on her skinny neck, the manager made her question a challenge.

Carialle shook her head. "Cleaning is cleaning."

"Good attitude. Peters will give you the necessary training for anything hazardous but I like to warn people. Saves my time and theirs. Had more than one pass out the first time a patient threw up or hemorrhaged in front of them." The amused expression came and went, apparently amusement over the delicate sensibilities of certain former employees. "You're off at seven in the morning. Report at six tomorrow night. I may need you to cover in a few day shifts, assuming you work out— will the odd schedule be a problem?"

"Of course not. Any time you need me I'll be here. I'm so grateful for the opportunity."

Gretta gave her a perfunctory smile and left the room without further comment.

Dak Peters was a gangly balding man of indeterminate age, friendly enough but anxious, with nervous tics.

The night passed quickly, as exhausted as Carialle was from the events of the day. She managed to keep up with Peters, while influencing him to think she was efficient and exactly what he needed in a staffer. Gretta checked on her twice, once watching her clean a visitors' bathroom for fifteen minutes or so. The manager provided no feedback or instructions but nodded in silent satisfaction as Carialle burnished the fixtures with a final swipe of her cloth.

She met the other night staff as she was making rounds with Peters and again in the dressing room at the end of the shift, but no one was inclined to chat. Co-workers who kept to themselves and clearly wanted to leave as fast as possible after work rather than bond over chitchat were exactly what she preferred, making the job even more perfect for her situation.

Walking home in the early morning light, she reflected on her new place of employment. There were three wings to the clinic. On one side were patients of all ages, in varying degrees of recovery from surgery or serious medical conditions. In the center was an urgent care establishment. In both areas, the nursing staff projected a caring and professional attitude, and their auras held the sunny yellow and positive pink of those who heal.

The third wing was much different, housing nine men, most of them elderly, all of them heavily sedated or nearly catatonic. She'd been shocked when Peters led her there, as it was such a contrast to the rest of the clinic. As soon as she'd crossed the threshold and the heavy door shut behind her, Carialle felt trapped, struggling to quell a sudden panic attack. One staffer sat at a console in the center. At first she naively assumed the man was monitoring the patients' vital signs until she realized he was watching a video on his AI that Carialle recognized as hard core porn, having seen Dobkin pleasure himself to the same scenes more than once.

Surprised, she scanned the man's aura and found the gray and sickly green hues of cruelty, greed and other negative traits tainting most in the Combine ranks. What was such a person doing in charge of desperately ill patients?

"Matikian, this is the new janitor," Peters said as they walked by. "You'll probably see her a lot."

Matikian raised one hand but didn't take his eyes off the vid screen. "Don't bother me, I won't bother you," was all he said.

"Who are these patients?" she asked as she toured the rooms with the supervisor.

"Former soldiers. Mrs. Trang has a contract with the planetary veterans' administration, to care for them." Peters gave her a look she couldn't interpret.

"How fortunate for them," she said, hoping she'd chosen an appropriate response. Peters relaxed so she decided she'd identified the correct tone to take. Carialle scanned the man whose room she was in and caught…nothing. Shocked, she tried again and found only gray. He might as well be dead. Yet the machines indicated he was alive. Each room was the same story. She squared her shoulders and stifled the questions flooding her mind. This was none of her business.

Reaching her new home, she took off the gray tunic and leggings and sprawled on her bare mattress in her utilitarian underwear. After four endless years of grinding captivity, she'd escaped, found a home and a job all in one day. Her good fortune seemed nearly too good to be true, especially given the undeniable truth her god had ignored all her previous pleas for help. *He must have intervened on my behalf today, but why?* The sudden generosity from the deity made her wary—what price would he place on his help? What might she be asked to do in return? Thuun was a just and fair god, or so the legends said, but he had high expectations of his priestesses. *Lucky I never officially became one.* Carialle decided to worry about Thuun's demands when the time came, closed her eyes and willed herself to fall asleep.

CHAPTER TWO

Around noon she awoke and made herself get dressed, trying to ignore the raging hunger in her belly. A bag of greasy munchies and stale cookies in the employee break room at the clinic were all she'd eaten since the late lunch the day before. She had to buy the shoes Gretta wanted her to wear, she needed basic amenities to make the apartment more livable and she definitely needed to shop for food. All before she reported to the clinic to start her next shift that evening.

When she ventured into the main courtyard on her way to the marketplace, she found Mrs. Galaganos on her knees, weeding a flowerbed, while an aged furry pet of indeterminate species dozed in the sun by her side. The landlady paused in her efforts as Carialle walked past. "Get the job?"

"Yes, thank you for the recommendation."

"How was Mrs. Trang?"

"I didn't meet her —she wasn't in. The manager, Gretta, hired me."

"Gretta's a good girl, local, knew her since she was a knee-high kid. I figured she'd like the looks of you, all soft spoken and deferential." Mrs. Galaganos struggled to rise and after a moment's hesitation, Carialle stepped across the flowers to help. "Thank you, sweetie. Off to do your shopping, are you?"

"I need a few things before going to work tonight."

As her landlady gently quizzed her about what she needed and made suggestions, Carialle used her power to peer more deeply into the woman's aura. The colors indicated Mrs. Galaganos liked to keep her fingers on everything going on in the neighborhood. She had a deep thirst for knowledge as a means of control of her environment. Living in a place like this, Carialle could see why the woman wanted to keep up with the business of everyone in her orbit. Knowledge was power in certain situations. She wondered if Mrs. Galaganos planned to pump her for gossip from the clinic. *If she gets too nosy about me, I'll have to be on the move.*

"You certainly maintain the garden in great shape," she said, trying to change the subject.

Pride evident on her face, Mrs. Galaganos surveyed her small domain. "Yes, all but the biggest tree. I'll be devastated if anything happens to it but the leaves have been dropping for ten days now and this isn't the leaf-casting season. I gave it extra water."

Impatient as she was to be off about her own errands, Carialle felt a compulsion to react to the concern about the possibly ailing tree. Tulavarrans and nature worked hand in hand on her planet and a priestess was never to ignore the needs of the differently-sentient. "Additional irrigation isn't always the best tactic," she said, walking toward the tree in question. "Let me take a look."

Mrs Galaganos trailed behind her. The pet yawned, rolled over in its patch of sun, and ignored them.

The tree had a beautiful shape, with a swirling trunk rising twenty feet in the air, and graceful branches currently sporting rather patchy clumps of leaves. The older leaves were a glossy deep green but the newer ones were shriveled, mottled with red and brown. Carialle stepped across the ornamental barrier of white shells and rested her hand on the tree, reaching for the sentient with her power. A carving to the left caught her eye. "What's this?"

"My late husband planted this tree when we moved in here, all those years ago." Mrs. Galaganos sighed. "He was such a romantic—he carved our names into the trunk, with a heart, in honor of our love. Said it represented our promise to each other. This tree is my last link to him—he died a year ago. I'll be devastated if it dies too. I feel close to him when I'm out here gardening in the shade of the tree." Her voice quavered and Carialle feared the elderly lady was on the verge of tears.

She peered more closely at the inscription and could barely make out two names and several slashes resembling a date. The heart shape was distorted by the tree's growth pattern. "It's lovely," she said, repressing a shudder at the idea of defacing the living wood in this fashion. The carving was old and clearly not the cause of the tree's current health problem. "Bugs. Living deep within the trunk, feasting on the rising sap."

"How—how can you tell?"

"I know a lot about plants. I've studied them." Carialle improvised. The tree was attempting to tell her what course of action might help it fight off the infestation. She sent the entity a comforting thought and then used her power to *push* the insects.

Mrs. Galaganos screeched and retreated as a flood of tiny black and white insects came pouring from the ground between the tree's gnarled roots, and out of every knothole. "I'll get the watering robo and drown them!" She hobbled to take action, as the pet arrived to growl and make threatening noises at the invaders. His elderly mistress washed the horde off the sidewalk and into a drain, muttering imprecations against them and obviously taking great joy in defeating the hitherto unseen enemy. Carialle bit her lip hard to repress her urge to grin at the landlady's enthusiasm.

She stepped away from the tree, hopping across the puddles and rivulets left behind on the sidewalk by Mrs. Galaganos's flood. "I believe if you sprinkle a spice which possesses a heavy concentration of capsaicin or a similar substance, around the roots once a week, work it into the ground with a trowel and then water, the tree will remain insect-free and should recover. Follow the procedure for four weeks."

"It looks better already."

Carialle pivoted on her heel to survey the tree. The leaves did seem healthier and the branches were less droopy.

"How—how did you do that?" Mrs. Galaganos was staring at her.

Hastily Carialle sent a thread of her power to calm the old woman, and to help her believe the lie she was about to utter. "I heard them moving and chirping under the bark and so I thumped hard on the tree. I guess I startled a bunch of them and the others followed, like larger creatures stampeding. You took care of the problem then."

Mrs. Galaganos took a deep breath and patted the robo by her side. "I certainly did."

With reluctance Carialle left an outsized feeling of gratitude for her efforts in her landlady's mind. The woman made it her business to know everyone and everything in the district apparently and Carialle might need a favor or significant help at some point. Always good to have a kernel of obligation already planted. "I've got to be going now. I'm running out of time before I have to be at work so I must get my errands done."

"See you later, dearie."

She waved and left the courtyard, heading for the marketplace. She'd probably gone overboard with her assistance to the tree, but it was hard to tamp down her power once she was engaged in a task actually proper and in line with her beliefs. At the same time, leaving Mrs. Galaganos feeling so indebted to her made her feel queasy. Uncomfortably close to the type of coercion the Combine had forced her to do.

The square wasn't as crowded today and Carialle was surprised how exposed and vulnerable she felt. The euphoria of yesterday over being a free woman had faded and more practical realities were setting in. As she hastened to the shoe store, she speculated whether Dobkin's body had been found yet and if anyone was hunting for her as a result. The Combine had the best technology, including image jammers, so she knew there'd be no usable surveillance video of the two of them anywhere. Dobkin kept his personal unit activated at all times, which had also protected her. But what about eye witnesses? Had anyone in the seedy hotel paid attention to Dobkin and his alien companion?

Not much I can do about any of it now. Just keep my head down and try to stay out of sight.

She was nearly late to work, which would have been disastrous for the second day on the job. Not only that but she'd barely made it into the changing room when Gretta appeared.

"Mrs. Trang is here today. She wants to interview you," the manager said. "Hurry up, finish dressing." She waited while Carialle hastily donned her blue clinic uniform and fastened the new work shoes. Then Gretta hustled her into the hall and took her to the administrative annex, where she'd not been before.

"Any advice for me?" Carialle asked, trying not to wince at the way her new shoes pinched her toes. There'd be blisters by morning, she was sure.

"She's all business so be concise in your answers." Gretta glanced at her. "I told her what a good job you did last night and Peters also put in a good word."

"Thank you."

"I wouldn't mention Mrs. Galaganos, not unless she asks you. The two of them don't get along too well. It's an old story."

Reading her companion's emotions, Carialle picked up the hint Mrs. Trang was afraid her employees might gossip with the old lady about patients or other clinic matters. Apparently Gretta had come close to losing her job at one point for talking too freely to the garrulous landlady.

"Here we are." Gretta paused at an imposing door, took a deep breath, brushed the creases from her already crisp jacket, and knocked. The portal swung open and the manager said, "I've brought our new probationary employee, as you asked, Mrs. Trang. This is Carialle Smith."

As Carialle advanced into the well-appointed office, her pulse raced. The stern woman facing her from behind a massive desk was one of those humans lucky enough to be genetically immune to her powers. Carialle would be able to read her basic aura but not to exert any influence over Mrs. Trang. She wasn't invited to sit, so she stood at attention, hands by her sides.

The door clicked shut. Evidently Gretta wasn't invited to join them.

"You have no papers, Miss Smith?"

"No." Carialle wasn't going to offer any explanation. She was hardly the only person in this district to be travelling off the grid.

"And Mrs. Galaganos sent you to us?" Trang sat perfectly quiet and composed, her hands clasped on the desk in front of her. She stared at Carialle as if she was equal parts bored and annoyed by having to interview a new employee.

"I rented an apartment there. I don't know her personally—I'm new to this district. But she did suggest I apply for a job here, as well as a few other places." Carialle stretched the truth a bit. "She was trying to be helpful." Not being able to use her powers to influence or compel others as she normally could was terrifying, like walking on a tiny bridge over a yawning abyss. She was annoyed at the anxiety making her pulse race but the clinic owner reminded her of the Combine bosses she'd met. Defiantly she sent a thread of her power out to read the woman's colors—gray, green, a hint of black. Not encouraging. But all she wanted from this person was a steady paycheck and no questions asked.

"My employees said you did a thorough job last night and were most respectful. Eager to learn."

"I'm glad they were pleased. I tried really hard." Carialle could make herself sound naïve and humble if required.

"Since this is a medical facility, the utmost discretion is required. We maintain absolute confidentiality about anything involving our patients, or of any procedures performed here, do you understand?"

"Perfectly. I'm just a janitor, Mrs. Trang, medical stuff goes over my head anyway. I want to do my job and earn my credits, nothing else."

Mrs. Trang was silent, her sculptured face giving nothing of her thoughts away.

Carialle forced herself not to fidget. *There are other jobs on this planet, after all.* She decided to risk a placating remark. "I don't want people discussing my personal business, so the last thing I'd ever do is betray confidences from my place of employment. You'll find I'm a loyal employee."

"Very well. You may remain here this week on probation, as Mrs. Nestrum explained to you. I'll leave it up to her to decide whether to keep you on or not after the week is up." Mrs. Trang leaned forward and pointed her right index finger at Carialle like a weapon. "If I hear of a single problem with your performance or any hint of your gossiping about my patients or my staff with your landlady, or anyone else, you'll be out. No second chances, understand?"

"Yes, ma'am. Thank you for taking a chance on me. I'm so grateful—"

"Don't fawn and don't babble. Get out."

Carialle fled, bumping into Gretta outside the door. The manager steadied her with one hand. "Our boss lady is in a class by herself, isn't she?"

"I never met anyone quite like her," Carialle agreed. Scary Mrs. Trang would fit right in at the Combine if she ever got tired of the medical field. "But she said I could keep the job, subject to your approval at the end of the week."

"Terrific. I expected as much. Well then, you have your cleaning assignment for the night, right?"

Carialle nodded her agreement. "I'll check with Peters if I finish early." *And I'll make a concerted effort not to be in Mrs. Trang's vicinity ever again.*

A week sped by, then two. The routine at the clinic wasn't taxing, since she didn't mind cleaning. Peters showed signs of finding her attractive, which she subtly repelled with her empathic gifts. Even then, he made excuses to seek her out and talk to her, which was disconcerting. This was her first encounter with an individual requiring repeated doses of her power to modify their behavior or emotion, much less their actions toward her personally. Apparently Peters' fixation on her ran deep. He didn't harass her, or try to touch her like Matikian did a few times, but his advances were an annoyance.

One of the military men on the closed ward died on her day off but since she didn't know any of the patients, Carialle wouldn't have been disturbed by the death, except for the odd colors flickering in the auras of certain employees. It was as if a few of the staff were relieved he'd died, or felt a degree of guilt about the death.

Others like Matikian had the green of greed mixed with the pale blue of eagerness. Carialle couldn't make sense of the conflicting emotions, unless the old man had left his favorites on the staff a few credits in his will. Since she'd never seen any of these patients in a conscious state, she wondered briefly how the deceased could have made such arrangements. Deciding it wasn't her problem, she pushed away the vague uneasiness caused by the attitude of her co-workers, chalking it up as another mystery of the gloomy vegetative patients' wing.

The man was elderly and in a hopeless vegetative state, and in due time he'd passed away, despite the excellent care. End of story.

Nothing to concern her.

Peters requested her to clean the now empty room first, including the medical equipment, which he'd begun to trust her with, in desperation after another orderly quit without giving notice.

"Of course, but what's the rush?" she asked.

"New patient coming tonight. Mrs. Trang will be here so I'd advise you to stay out of her way. She can be a bit abrupt when doing intake on a new person."

"After my job interview with her, I can easily believe she'd be brusque on every occasion—say no more."

Hoping to avoid the owner, Carialle rushed to the now empty room and was finishing the last touches when she heard a commotion outside. Hastily she gathered up her tools and supplies and directed her robo cart into the corridor. Coming toward her was Mrs. Trang, talking to an officious man dressed all in white, while behind them was an anti grav litter escorted by four husky orderlies. Peters and Matikian trailed behind. The patient on the litter was shouting incoherently, fighting the restraints, cursing. He seemed to be in the grip of a delusion about being captured by Mawreg, the deadliest enemy of the Sectors civilization, against whom war was constantly being waged.

Appalled both by the man's violent behavior and the cruel way he was restrained, Carialle flattened herself against the wall and watched as the litter was floated into the room, rocking precariously from the vehement struggles of the ill man. It took all four of the attendants to transfer him to the bed and shackle him tightly to the rails, as Peters slid the medical unit over the lower half of the patient's body. Matikan jabbed an inject into the man's neck with a force that made Carialle wince. *He enjoyed that.*

The patient convulsed and collapsed, going limp against his bonds.

"I'd keep him well under control," the man in charge said. "Fully sedated. For his own good," he added with a wink.

"Yes, doctor, of course." Mrs. Trang was all smiles as she agreed with the suggested course of treatment.

Carialle was shocked to find the owner's aura full of the bright green of greed, banded with the rusty red of evil and the corroded gold of improperly used power. She lingered to watch the patient as the others left the room, inhaling sharply as her still active senses 'read' him.

At his core was the blue fire of a true warrior of Thuun. His aura blazed with it.

Small patches of the dull gray intruded around the edges of the flames, probably from the inject he'd been given. The flames were distorted in a disturbing fashion she'd never seen before, blurry. Odd pools of oily black drifted in the center of his aura, three of them, walled off from each other by twisted knots of bright white so glaring she had to shut down her observation, which had never happened to her before.

"Hey, you ok?"

She jumped as Peters tapped her shoulder. "Sorry, I—I was surprised at how agitated the man was when he was brought him in."

"Yeah, the patients are usually a lot farther gone by the time we get them. He's a big prize."

"What do you mean?" Disturbed by her vision of the blue flames, as well as those mysterious black pools confined by the white lights, Carialle kept walking toward the next area she was due to clean. *Mustn't appear to be slacking off, especially with the owner on the premises.*

"Sweetie, what do you think Mrs. Trang is running here?" Peters kept pace with her.

Puzzled, she said, "A rehab clinic."

He shook his head. "Yeah sure, in the other part of the building. Over here, she keeps them alive so she can scrape their veterans' benefits. And she takes the payments for all the fancy therapy, nutritious foods, supplemental meds and special care they're supposed to be receiving. Nice little racket. Her and the doc are in it together. He directs suitable patients her way and she gives him a kickback." Peters leaned closer, as if the way to her reluctant heart was to share his employer's secrets with her. "This new guy ain't even supposed to be here. He was Special Forces, badly injured in action, then got himself tortured by the Mawreg before he was rescued. The military ran him through rejuve regeneration to fix his body but his mind is fucked up. He was supposed to go to a fancy, high end rehab clinic on the eastern continent but Trang and the doc diverted him here. Forged the records. No one will ever know he existed. Much less find him."

"Why?" Horrified, she exerted pressure to keep him talking for once. This new patient wasn't her problem, not at all, but the glimpse of the blue flames rattled her to the core. Assisting a warrior of Thuun was the highest duty of a priestess. *But I'm not a priestess and he can't be a warrior of my god—he's human. I don't know him, I owe him nothing.* But despite her frantic denials, she was under a compulsion to understand the situation more fully.

"Special Forces are awarded a more generous pension than these other poor bastards who were regular military, maybe five times as much. What she really wants from our new resident though is his veterans' acres. He's entitled to prime real estate, courtesy of the grateful Sectors."

"How will she acquire land meant to be his?"

"The drug she gives them, toranquidol? It destroys the mind over time but there's a point in the process where free will is gone but the victim retains certain functions. She can make them do anything she wants. She's gotten rich off of having these poor bastards change their wills, sign over property, you name it. Even married one or two of them along the way for the death benefit and life insurance payouts. He'll sign the forms to give her the veterans acres." Peters chuckled, sounding as if he admired Mrs. Trang's ingenuity at scamming. "I guess what the Sectors authorities don't know won't hurt them. I mean, who cares, right?"

"But don't the patients' families—"

Peters shook his head. "She and the doc pick their targets carefully. No family, no one to ask awkward questions. Or interfere."

An orderly was walking down the hall toward them so Carialle bit her lip and compelled Peters to forget he'd told her anything. She parted ways with her chatty supervisor at the next fork in the corridor and avoided him and all the other employees the rest of the night. The areas she was assigned to clean sparkled more brightly than ever as Carialle tried to stop her thoughts from wandering to what Peters had told her by scrubbing and polishing as if the area was about to be inspected by Mrs. Trang.

On the way out of the building after changing into her own clothing, she overheard Matikian on a personal com call, gloating to whoever he was speaking with about how the bonus he'd get for managing this new patient's care would be his biggest yet.

Did he cause the last patient's death at Trang's command perhaps? Is that why he had greed in his aura? Does Mrs. Trang reward him for taking an active role in defrauding these poor men? Carialle repressed a wave of nausea and gave Matikian a casual wave as he glanced at her. He frowned and swiveled his chair in the other direction, lowering his voice as he continued to talk.

When she reached the sanctuary of her apartment building, she took a few moments to refresh her powers, lingering in the garden to pull energy from the plants and the planet slumbering below. She chatted with her landlady about trivialities for a few moments while they pulled weeds together and trimmed a few deadhead blooms from the flowering bushes. She checked on the all-important tree Mrs. Galaganos's late husband had planted and was relieved to find it doing well, much stronger now the bugs had fled. New leaf shoots were appearing.

She escaped into her small space soon thereafter. Even though she accepted the fact the lodging was temporary and she'd have to leave probably sooner than later, she'd taken delight in fixing the place up a bit with colorful fabric for the curtains and tablecloth, and interesting bits and pieces from the local marketplace. Nothing too expensive, nothing showy. Her pay from the clinic wasn't generous and her hoard of credits grew slowly. But after four long years as a prisoner, held in a grim gray cell, she delighted in even tiny opportunities to express herself and revel in colors and patterns.

Changing into one of her new, gauzy cotton dresses, Carialle brewed a cup of tea in the chipped mug she'd rescued from a pile of things left by a departing tenant. She'd been drawn to the whimsical depiction of feline animals under the glaze. Walking across the soft green-and-blue floral carpet remnant she'd also acquired, she sat on the bed, holding the mug between her hands. Against her will she saw the vision of the new patient, fighting his bonds, full of desire to live and rage at his captors.

"It's not my battle," she said out loud. "This isn't Tulavarra." But she had a sinking feeling she'd be drawn further into the situation anyway. Why else would Thuun direct her here, make finding a home and a job so simple, place her at the clinic, if not to help one of his warriors? Leaning against the pillows, she let the empty mug fall to the carpet and closed her eyes. *This choice is unfair—I have my own life to live, my own difficulties. I've suffered enough.*

The next evening she was assigned to clean in the general wing of the clinic but the night after she was back in the veterans' area. The new arrival's room was last on her schedule. As she and her robo cart entered the room, she was relieved to see he lay as motionless as all the others, although he was securely restrained at the wrists and ankles. The medical unit delivering nutrients and fluids to his body and removing wastes hummed quietly as it did its work, positioned over his abdomen and groin, covering him to the knees.

Taking a nervous glance over her shoulder, even though she knew Matikian wouldn't leave his chair at the central console, where he was occupied with his favorite vids, she stepped to the bed.

"Marcus Valerian." She read his name from the settings on the medic unit, liking the sound of the syllables. The name suited him. She studied what was visible of his nude body, well-muscled, sturdy. No scars or tattoos but she supposed the marks had been eliminated in the regeneration process. His face was handsome, with a strong jaw and high cheekbones. At well over six feet tall, he had the look of a formidable soldier. His muscles would inevitably atrophy as he was kept in the bed, drugged into a motionless stupor and the realization bothered her on his behalf. Marcus must have worked hard to maintain his body.

The beds were equipped with sensors and tech to prevent bed sores and to keep the skin clean, but the process was more for the benefit of the staff and Mrs. Trang than the patients'. Less care required if the body stayed healthy externally. In Carialle's time at the clinic she'd never seen any physical therapy performed on the ex-military patients.

She'd done a little research earlier in the day on the cheap AI she'd bought refurbished at the marketplace and watched a popular trideo drama about a Special Forces team. Truly these men and women were incredible warriors, capable of nearly miraculous feats. Unable to stop herself, she touched Marcus's arm, stroking her palm over his skin from cuffed wrist to elbow in a gesture meant to be comforting even as she scanned his aura. With her touch, she transferred a bit of healing power. "You'd hate what they're doing to you," she whispered. The blue flames at his core were still vivid to her eyes, although there were more patches of the dull gray intruding. The meds were working quickly. *Maybe Mrs. Trang ordered a higher dose.*

But his conscious mind, his sense of self, was already gone, wasn't that what Peters had said? Broken under alien torture? Maybe this was actually a mercy, finishing his days in a drugged peace.

But she had a hard time accepting the conclusion. Having been kept in chains herself, as a prisoner of the Combine, she was revolted to see another sentient treated so.

Time to clean and get out. Carialle stepped away from the bed to get her supplies, and rubbed her aching lower back, trying to work out the kinks. It had been a long time since she first labored as a maid at the temple, and she wasn't getting any younger. Smiling to herself, because she was far from being an old woman, she turned, tools in hand, and froze.

Marcus Valerian was awake and staring at her. His eyes were blue, the same blue as the flames burning inside his soul. He licked his chapped lips and strained one wrist against the padded restraints, as if reaching for her. "Where?" he whispered. "What…planet?"

"Felicia Seven."

"Home." He let his head fall onto the skinny pillow and closed his eyes again.

Nerves making her dizzy, she gave the room a cursory cleaning and escaped. She debated mentioning to Matikian how the soldier had awakened for a brief moment but held her tongue. Reluctance to betray the fact made silence the wiser course to follow, especially as no one ever seemed to care about the details of the patients' health on this wing. No one expected her to report on a patient's physical condition.

Marcus struggled through layers of thick, gluelike fog, striving to wake up, to open his eyes. He felt as if he was cocooned in webs. A heavy weight lay across his hips and groin and he could feel the unpleasant cold of nutrients entering his system through some kind of tube, while embarrassingly the damn machine was also removing bodily wastes through other tubes. *What the seven fucking hells is going on here?* He tried to raise one hand to his forehead and discovered with a rush of adrenaline he was in tight restraints, unable to move or defend himself.

Incredulous, he lay against the pillow, studying the room while he controlled his breathing. It was unlike any military hospital he'd ever been in and although it was hard to search, tethered as he was, there was no call button anywhere on the bed to summon help. No vital signs monitor either, he realized as he became more alert. No vid or com unit on the wall or ceiling.

Nothing to look at but the cracks in the ceiling. Not even a window. Just him and a bed and the damn intrusive machine hooked up to his body.

His first instinct was to yell for a nurse or a doctor, anyone with the ability to get him out of this uncomfortable setup, but no one responded to his demands. His voice was weaker than he was used to and his muscles trembled a bit from the effort he was making. Marcus studied the restraints on his wrists, which weren't like anything he'd ever seen before, and could find no way out, despite his military training.

How long have I been here?

He replayed his tattered memories and the last clear thing he could recall was being severely injured, crawling through an overgrown jungle toward the medevac point, dragging a buddy who was probably already dead. And then—He screwed his eyes shut tight.

And then the Mawreg had found him and taken him prisoner. He could not, would not remember what happened after he was captured. But he must have had hope of rescue, because he hadn't activated the checkout code implant in his mind which brought instant death.

This place sure wasn't heaven.

Although it might be hell.

There were vague hints in his memories indicating he'd spent time on a Sectors hospital ship, he thought, possibly even treated in a rejuve resonator. But he couldn't be sure since he knew for a fact he'd been treated twice before after severe injuries suffered in earlier missions. His mind was fuzzy—whatever drug they were giving him was screwing with his mental processes.

Maybe this was a trap. Maybe he remained trapped in the Mawreg labs, undergoing mental torture of some kind.

A man appeared in the doorway, holding an inject. "Awake, are we? Time for your next dose, soldier boy."

"I'm Captain Marcus Valerian, Sectors Special Forces, and I demand to speak to whoever is in charge here," he said, infusing as much command into his tone as he could manage. The man's dismissive attitude infuriated him. "There's clearly been a mistake."

"Right now I'm in charge and you don't get to make demands," the newcomer said, advancing to the bed. "Let me give you more of the magic sleep juice and whatever you're worried about won't matter in a few minutes, I promise. A few more days under our tender care and you won't even be waking up to talk about it."

Marcus resisted the shot as best he could, being in severe restraint, but the orderly clamped his hand around Marcus's upper arm and jabbed the applicator into a vein. As soon as the drug hit his system his hold on reality slithered away from him in a tidal wave of warm dizziness.

The attendant laughed. "Told you it was good stuff. High street value but free for you. You can thank me later." He patted Marcus on the shoulder and moved to check on the medunit, adjusting a control here and there.

"You've got no right to hold me," Marcus said, although the words came out garbled. His head was spinning and the periphery of his vision grew black.

One final memory swam out of the darkness into his mind's eye. A beautiful woman, with skin the color of pale jade and emerald green eyes holding a hint of gold in their lustrous depths. She'd told him he was home. If he was going to escape this predicament, he needed her help and he prayed to the Lords of Space he'd see her again. *I hope she was real.*

CHAPTER THREE

The next night when Carialle came onto the floor, she heard yelling and swearing. With a sinking feeling in her stomach, she realized the uproar had to be coming from Marcus. She was astounded to find Matikian unperturbed, sitting at the console as usual.

"Shouldn't you go see what's wrong?" she asked timidly, glancing in the direction of the noise.

"I know what's wrong, poor deluded bastard wants to be uncuffed. Thinks he can leave." The orderly laughed. "Yeah, only way he's leaving will be on a stretcher, as cold meat, straight to the boneyard." Looking at her as she hesitated, he said, "Clean his room last if the noise upsets you. I'll give him his next dose in half an hour and then he'll be quiet. Day shift had a problem with him too. Only with them he was having flashbacks to his time in the Mawreg experimentation camp. "

"Thank you," she said, the anger in her heart over the man's treatment like a hot coal burning. If he needed his meds, they shouldn't be withheld. She debated using her power to get Matikian to give Marcus the inject now, but since she had her doubts about the medicine, she couldn't force herself to intercede. She cleaned the first room, clenching her teeth against the continuing tirade from down the hall and debating what—if anything—was proper for her to do.

Before going into the second patient's room, she tiptoed to the threshold of Marcus's and peeked inside. He was thrashing in the bed, fighting the restraints, attempting to throw the med unit off his lower body with violent movements. *Maybe I shouldn't have told him where he is. Maybe it would have been better to let him remain ignorant.*

The sounds stopped as he caught sight of her. Wide shoulders raised as far as the restraints would allow, the soldier stared at her. "Please," he said softly.

"Come to gawk at the wild beast?" Matikian shouldered her aside. "He's quite a fine specimen all right." He advanced into the room, holding up the inject. "I've got what you need right here, buddy, keep you quiet, let the maid and me get our work done in peace."

Marcus cursed him loudly, using words Carialle had never heard before, even from the worst of the Combine's thugs. Matikian laughed, easily evading the attempt Marcus made to bite him and jabbed the inject into the patient's arm. "Double dose tonight, pal. Enjoy it while you still have a brain cell left."

Unable to watch any longer, Carialle fled. She spent a few minutes in the bathroom, crying from emotional overload, and then emerged into the corridor to go on with her duties. She had to keep her job no matter how distressing the circumstances.

Matikian was waiting, leaning on the wall. "You ok?"

She sent a quick tendril of her power towards him. As she'd suspected, he wasn't asking out of any concern for her, but only to gauge if she was going to make trouble for him. "I'm sorry if I made your job harder tonight," she said humbly, the lies ashes in her mouth. She'd spoken similar falsehoods to bullies in power before. "I—I shouldn't have gone to look at the patient before you dosed him. It upset him more, didn't it? I mean, you warned me and you're the boss." Technically he wasn't her boss but she needed to boost his ego. "Please don't report me to Peters."

Matikian grinned and gave her a side hug, fingers brushing against her breast, which she endured, biting her lip. "Of course not. The patient's quite amusing when he's all riled up with nowhere to go. I get it. You and me—we're all good. You can clean his room anytime you like now." Giving her a pat on the butt, he swaggered to the console.

Carialle took a deep breath, nauseous at the idea of treating Marcus or anyone like a wild animal to be gawked at. Matikian had quite a streak of sadism in his makeup. She hadn't missed the way he jabbed the inject into the helpless man's arm, forcing it to hurt despite the built-in safeguards. She hadn't missed other bruises on Marcus's body either. The orderly must not fear any retribution from Mrs. Trang, should she come for a surprise inspection, and what did his confidence in his attitude to abuse the patients say about the clinic owner? It certainly supported what Peters had told her about why Mrs. Trang ran this place.

She cleaned all the other rooms and areas and then tiptoed into Marcus's, reluctant to speak to him, hoping he was unconscious so she'd be spared any more pressure to intervene. The less she knew of him, the better for her own safety.

But the cowardly inclination sat uncomfortably in her mind. Since when was she afraid to do what was right?

Since the Amarotu Combine made her a slave.

She stood beside the bed for a moment, staring at the soldier's face. His brow was furrowed even under the drug's influence and his hands were fisted against the rails. Reluctantly she checked his wrist restraints, alarmed at the dried blood staining the edges. He'd fought so hard. Reaching into her pocket, she fumbled for her hand lotion, since dry hands were a fact of life as a maid. She rubbed a dollop on the part of his wrist she could reach under the tight restraint and then crossed to the other side of the bed and repeated the effort, hoping to soothe his raw skin. As she worked the lotion into his wrists, she hummed a blessing song, sending him a smidgen of restorative power.

She examined his aura, trying to ascertain the soundness of his mind and personality. The flames were less distorted, had other positive colors twining through them, although the gray was eating into the edges at a surprising speed. *I don't think he's insane or broken, any more than I am.* Perhaps he had been at one time, maybe the powerful tranquilizers had given him a respite for his mind to heal itself. And maybe her brief interventions, like this one tonight, sending him a small dose of her power as a gift, had helped. She was no formally educated healer, no trained priestess, but she knew how to wield her gifts.

But was it truly a blessing to heal him, if he was doomed to lie in this bed until Dr. Trang had what she wanted and killed him?

Nervously glancing at the door, she tightened her grasp on his fingers, because physical contact amplified her power, and she sent her senses arrowing into the core of where the blue flames, the black pools and the white lights met in his mind.

A second later she reeled back, gasping. The black pools contained such awful thoughts and emotions under their oily surface that she could understand why the poor man ranted and raved at times. How he could display any sanity at all baffled her. She leaned on the foot of the bed, breathing hard, considering what she'd seen. There were completely alien elements in the depths of the black, colors she had no name for. Could his enemy captors have implanted things in his mind? Were the white light strands his unconscious, desperate attempt to wall off the infestation, in order to function and survive?

Biting her lip, she stepped to the bedside again and forced herself to reach for his hand. Marcus's fingers curled around hers ever so slightly, although she didn't believe he truly knew she was there. Closing her eyes, she studied the black pools with her senses, leaving herself dangerously unprotected against discovery by Matikian or Peters. There were three of the alien deposits inside Marcus's aura. She picked the largest and sent her gift against it, injecting the area with her brightest colors of hope while the oil pulsed and shrank under the assault. Next she unbraided the tightly woven white strands Marcus's mind had apparently used to defend himself. The lights were tangled and lumpy but eventually she'd combed them into fine silk ribbons with her mental 'fingers', then watched in amazement as the slender filaments launched themselves like lightning bolts at the two remaining pools of black.

Shaking, knees buckling after the amount of energy she'd exerted, Carialle lost her grip on his hand and sank to the floor. No more would be possible tonight, not for her. Perhaps his own energies could wage a battle against the alien implants now. She'd never seen such things in all her time at the temple on Tulavarra and honestly she hoped she never saw the like again. Who were these Mawreg, to be able to force a warrior like Marcus to endure such unheard of torment? The Shemdylann who'd attacked her world and kidnapped her and her fellow Tulavarrans were frightening enough but these Mawreg must truly be the monsters spoken of in the oldest legends.

Her activities had bumped against other searing memories in his soul during the session, but those were real, human reactions to combat and related events of war. She couldn't heal those in this manner—Marcus's active participation and willingness to confront and work through the stress fractures would be required. But when it came to the alien colors, her powers rose to the occasion willingly. Eagerly.

Grabbing the bed rail, she dragged herself to her feet. This room was going to have to remain less than perfectly cleaned tonight. She'd no strength left for scrubbing, although the robo had done its surface cleaning untended while she fought her battle for Marcus's mind.

"I hope I did the right thing for you," she said, staring at his face, unable to decide if he looked more at peace now.

Brushing his hair off his forehead, she sighed and went to accomplish her remaining tasks in the veterans' wing as best she could.

She spent her next day off researching veterans' affairs as best she could but was unable to find anyone she could anonymously try to involve on Marcus's case. With dismay, she recognized the doctor who worked with Mrs. Trang as being the authority in charge of the planet's veterans' affairs agency and it certainly wasn't going to do any good to send him a whistle blower note. Attempting to learn more about Sectors Special Forces was also a dead end, as all aspects of information about them seemed to be classified, other than promo about their successful missions. Unlike other branches of the planetary and Sectors military, they didn't even recruit directly. She was left with no idea who could be safely contacted about a veteran diverted to the wrong hospital.

And the police weren't even worth considering. How many times had she heard the Combine members boast of all the planets where the cops were on their payroll? No, she couldn't take a chance, risking herself and probably Marcus. A person as nefarious as Mrs. Trang appeared to be undoubtedly had ties to the Combine. As far as she could tell from the news reports, the Combine hadn't reconstituted itself after the big takedown the SCIA had pulled off, but even if Dobkin was dead, there were elements of the mob syndicate remaining on this planet, including the man he'd called before his fatal fall. That person was aware he'd had a Combine asset with him and might search for her. An organization as evil as this one would regenerate from the ashes, no matter what the Sectors did to root them out. She had to remain under their scanners.

Carialle looked at her now cozy apartment and bit her lip. Soon it would be time to move on, find a new place to hide. She wished she had more credits but it was dangerous for her to settle in one place too long. She had to stay ahead of whoever might come to find and recapture her.

She fled outside to the garden and worked with the plants for a few hours, allowing nature to sooth her soul and calm her anxieties over attempting to root the alien interference from Marcus's mind, the Combine and what else, if anything, she should do for the new patient.

Reporting for work that night her stomach was in knots, apprehensive over how Marcus was faring.

"You missed fireworks today after lunch, Mrs. Trang was here and she was not happy," Peters told Carialle as she headed toward the dressing room. "Seems someone is asking awkward questions about where Marcus Valerian ended up after he was shipped home."

For a tense moment she feared maybe her own inquiries had created the problem but then she realized the impossibility. She'd done nothing where his name had been mentioned. "His friends in the military maybe?"

"Maybe. So far there's been nothing concrete but she's upset he's not further along with the toranquidol regimen. She thinks maybe all the military implants and stuff are retarding the effects. Special Forces guys get loaded up with secret gear and special injects," Peters said. "She tripled his dose. Once he reaches the compliant stage in a day or two, and signs off on giving her his veteran's acres deed, he'll probably have a convenient stroke and die. Now she thinks he's too much potential trouble to keep going for the monthly benefits. Probably for the best. If the clinic was to get investigated, we'd all be in trouble." He gave her a meaningful look, right eyebrow raised and she realized he was subtly warning her. She'd have to flee on short notice or find herself in legal jeopardy. "No one cares much about the cases we usually get assigned," he said. "This guy is different in too many ways, starting with his being from the Special Forces."

"Thanks for the heads up." Carialle forced herself to smile as she entered the dressing room and Peters continued on his way with a cheery wave. She sank onto the bench in front of her locker and rubbed her forehead. *What to do now?* She knew the answer, plain as day, she was just trying to avoid admitting it to herself. She had to help the warrior escape—it was Thuun's highest commandment for one with her power. One did not say to the god that Marcus wasn't of her people and therefore none of her business, when so plainly Thuun had swayed events to place her here.

And how many times did I wish someone would step forward to help me and the other Tulavarran captives? I have to be that person for Marcus.

Checking for reassurance Matikian was deeply engrossed in his usual salacious entertainment, she cleaned one room and then another, knowing she was stalling. She took the robo cart and entered Marcus's room, moving to the bedside and searching for his aura at the same time. Was it her imagination or were the blue flames less vivid? Certainly there was more of the ominous gray. On the other hand, the pools of black had shrunk to mere shadows and were crisscrossed by white bands of light, so she believed he was well on the way to recovery from the alien experimentation. Taking a deep breath and glancing nervously over her shoulder, she pulled on her reserves of power and called to him to awaken. Fighting the drugs in his system was like wading through gritty mud and her skin crawled as she imagined the gray filth of the toranquidol touching her.

The bed shook as he startled in his restraints like a sleeping infant suddenly wakened, and she opened her eyes to see him staring at her. She held a finger to her lips and scurried to check the door. Satisfied Matikian was ignoring the world around him as usual, she hurried to the bedside and slid her fingers over Marcus's hand. Leaning close, she whispered, "I'm going to help you but we have to be careful, understand?"

His pupils were huge, dilated from the drugs. He tried to speak but no sound came out. Hastily she laid her hand across his chapped lips. "I'll ensure you get less of the medicine but you have to convince them you're still sedated. Can you put on an act?"

Marcus studied her face for a moment. "Yes." Getting the single syllable out seemed to require almost more energy than he possessed.

"Good. And then we'll see what we can do about getting you out of here."

"Today," he whispered against her hand. "Now."

"Not yet—you aren't ready. There's time. Trust me."

She removed her fingers and he spoke so faintly she had to shake her head and lean closer. His breath puffed against her ear as he repeated himself. "Angel."

Laughing, she shook her head. "Far from it, but I can't stand aside and let them do this to you. I'm going to send you under again but you'll remember our agreement." She released her hold on his consciousness and his eyelids drifted downward, despite his obvious struggle to stay awake.

To her astonishment, he shook his head, squared his shoulders and reopened his eyes. "Name?"

"Carialle."

Although he clearly was desperate to say more, his head lolled to the side and he snored as the drug took him.

Her adrenaline spiking from having made her risky decision and acted upon it, she did another rapid check of the hall, reassuring herself Matikian was oblivious. Then she took a deep breath and directed her power at the orderly, to create the impression he'd already administered today's dose to Marcus. After a few moments of her concentrated energy, Matikian leaned forward to make an entry in the console's AI database, and she relaxed.

So far, so good.

Carialle trudged off to clean the other rooms.

He woke in the morning feeling closer to normal than he had in months. Relieved, Marcus tried to move and the restraints bit into his painfully chafed wrists and ankles. *Right, still a prisoner in this hellhole.* But he felt unaccountably optimistic, even as he lay helpless and weak. Being forced to remain prone in one position and denied real food was affecting his readiness to take action. He flexed his hands and feet, then launched into the same isometric exercises he'd performed every time he was fortunate enough to be conscious. His wrists were a little less sore and as he moved, a delicate floral smell came to his nostrils, faint enough to be almost nonexistent. He remembered the encounter last night with Carialle. She was the reason he was better today. Apparently she'd carried out whatever her plan was to keep the monsters running this place from filling him with more of the damn drug, last night at least.

He wondered what she'd done. Would he see her again tonight? He pushed away a flicker of suspicion whether her kindness might be part of a larger psychological experiment being conducted on him. *Those eyes of hers are so beautiful, like gazing into her soul.* He refused to believe she was lying to him. But why was she helping him? She worked in this cursed place after all—she must have seen others treated as he was, or worse. What did she want from him in return? Taking risks like the ones she was running came at a high price. Well, he'd gladly pay, to get out of this hell.

Hearing voices in the hall, he closed his eyes and forced himself to relax. Remembering his promise to Carialle, he lay apparently unresponsive as two people entered his room and walked to stand beside the bed. Hoping his act was good enough to fool them, he was glad there were no vital signs monitors in the room because his heart was racing. Normally his heart rate slowed in a combat situation and he was deadly calm. His hard won Special Forces skills were taking a beating under the onslaught of the drugs and frustration at his own physical weakness roiled his gut.

"Guess the increased dose of toranquidol finally kicked in. He's not yelling obscenities this morning," said one voice. "Sleeping like a baby." A rough hand poked him in the ribs and he forced himself not to react.

"A few more days at this dose and he'll do anything Trang asks." The second person made an obscene suggestion about what service could be requested of Marcus and both sniggered. They riffed in this vein for a few more moments. He hoped the pair were making jokes at his expense, not speculating what the mysterious 'Trang' might actually do to him when he was sufficiently under mind control.

Wearying of the salacious banter at last, one of the orderlies finished with, "And then we'll be rid of him. I'm ready to reset to our usual patient load. No fuss, no muss."

"And no more shouting. Should we give him an extra shot? Hurry the process along?"

Marcus counted backward to keep himself from visibly tensing up at the idea of another inject of whatever poison was pumping into him. Carialle seemed to think it was essential he not be drugged for whatever escape attempt she had in mind to succeed. Considering how each inject wiped him out for hours, he agreed.

"Nah, Mrs. Trang calculated the dosages pretty carefully. She's going out of town for two days so if we push it and he passes through the compliant stage too fast, and goes brain dead before she can get her hands on the deed to his veteran's acres, it'll be our necks."

The men left the room and Marcus breathed a cautious sigh of relief. This was one precarious situation he was in and the mysterious Carialle was his only, scarily slender reed of hope. He set himself the task of feigning passivity for the remainder of the day, to keep lulling the suspicions of the staff imprisoning him.

When Carialle reported for duty that night, her stomach was in knots and she hadn't been able to eat dinner. She was terrified her impromptu plan would go wrong somehow and she only had one chance at rescuing Marcus. If she failed tonight, Trang and her employees would make sure the poor soldier was denied another opportunity to escape. She'd be lucky to escape herself if she messed this up.

The first hurdle was to see if he'd managed to stay unsedated all day. As she got ready to leave the dressing room, straightening her blue tunic, she remembered with a blush that he was naked. Going to the rack of uniforms, she took the largest one there and bundled it into a tightly folded square, hidden under her cleaning supplies. *Nothing I can do about shoes.* She stifled a nervous giggle. If his having to escape barefoot was her only problem tonight, they'd be doing fine.

Once she reached the ward, everything was reassuringly normal, although Peters was deeply engrossed in conversation with Matikian, debating about a local sports championship. Carialle forced herself to greet both men cheerfully and clean the first room, spending extra time on it, as she could hear the pair continuing their talk. She didn't want to expend shards of power encouraging Peters to leave but she would if the men chatted much longer. A few moments later the supervisor left on his own and she knew it was only the orderly, the comatose patients and herself in the wing.

Moving at her normal speed to make her motions unsuspicious and routine, if Matikian bothered to pay any attention to her movements, she bypassed the other rooms and entered Marcus's. He lay with his eyes closed and for a heart stopping moment she thought he must have been dosed during the day after all. *I can bring him to consciousness for a short time but not long enough, and not with the strength to walk.* She stood beside the bed, touched his bare shoulder gingerly and whispered his name.

Marcus snapped his eyes open, studying her face intently. "You came back."

"I said I would. How do you feel?"

He shrugged as best he could. "Woozy. Ready to get out of here. What's the plan, lady?"

"The first part is on me. I have to send Matikian, the orderly, to sleep. Then we get you loose and we run." She went to the door and took a quick peek into the hall. Taking a deep breath, she began to hum the song for lulling the harvested fields into a dormant state, which was the closest analogy she could think of, and built her power, launching an attack on her unsuspecting co-worker, compelling him to rest his head on the desk and sleep. As she watched, and sang her chant as quietly as she could, he nodded off. It looked as if he might fall so she rushed down the hall and guided him to a safe position, snoring. Carialle grabbed his control cards from his belt and ran to Marcus's room.

"All right, he's out." She hesitated, not sure where to begin freeing him.

"Restraints first," Marcus said.

Carialle fumbled with his right wrist, nerves making her clumsy. She could sense the tension in Marcus, saw how he kept biting his lip, probably to keep himself from snapping orders at her. He was constantly checking the door. "I'm sorry, I've never done this before," she said, trying to apologize and explain her lack of vital knowledge. "I'm not usually allowed to touch the patients."

"Take a deep breath, you're doing fine." His calm voice steadied her nerves.

She finally figured out how to insert the control card while simultaneously pressing the release button and the restraint snapped open. "Your poor wrist," she said, staring at the abraded, bloody marks.

"I've survived a lot worse." He made a fist and flexed his arm as if trying to reawaken the muscles. "Do the other one and then I can work on getting the damn machine off me while you free my ankles."

She was able to open the restraint for his left wrist rapidly and then they studied the medunit. "I think one of these controls it," she said uncertainly, fanning out the cards she held.

He held out his hand and she gave him the loop of keys, detaching the one she needed for his ankles. Sitting up a bit unsteadily, Marcus fumbled with the unit, and the ever present humming died as he managed to turn it off. With a stifled groan and a bitten off curse, he laid against the pillow.

"What's wrong?" Wringing her hands, unsure what to do, she rushed to the head of the bed. "What happened?"

"Fucking tubes…withdrawing…hurts like a sonofabitch." He bit his lip hard enough to draw blood and clenched his fists on the rails. "This is some lame cheap tech they've been using on me."

The medunit emitted a loud click and a beep and swung away from the bed. Involuntarily Carialle looked down to make sure he was all right and then hastily averted her eyes from his naked body. Other than more bruises, he seemed fine. And well endowed. Even in this crisis situation she couldn't help but notice. "Can you sit up?" Keeping her eyes scrupulously trained on his face, she braced him with her arm behind his back and was alarmed to feel muscle tremors as he strove to sit up.

"Am I escaping naked?" The tone was light but his grin was twisted, as if he was still in pain.

"Barefoot, not naked." She ran to the cart and pulled out the uniform she'd stolen earlier. As she handed it over, she heard unexpected noise in the hallway, Peters' voice as he tried to rouse Matikian.

"Fuck." Marcus slid off the bed, barely keeping himself upright.

"Get dressed. I'll handle this." Hoping the soldier could manage to stand long enough to put on the clothing, she grabbed her robo cart and walked into the hall, heading casually toward the console while her heart pounded in her chest. "Hey, Peters, what's wrong with Matikian?"

Hands on his hips, the supervisor frowned as he observed the snoring orderly. "I don't know. Drunk maybe. He was coherent and conscious when I was here before. Did you notice anything odd about him after I left?"

"No, he was his usual self." She lied with the most cheerful tone she could manage. "Let me know if you need help."

Entering the nearest room as if she was going to clean, Carialle leaned on the wall and hummed, building her power to send Peters to sleep as well. It was harder than the original effort because she hadn't been able to recharge her ability in between. A moment later she heard a thud as he too hit the floor. Fighting off a vision of Dobkin's death from a fall, she ran to the console, checking to see Peters was breathing, and then fled to see how Marcus was doing.

He was dressed in the one piece uniform, fabric stretched tight over his muscular frame, leaning on the bed, knuckles white with the effort to stay on his feet. Turning his head as she rushed in, he said, "Adrenaphix."

The word made no sense to her. "What?"

"I need a hit of adrenaphix."

"What is that?"

"An energy boost. We use it all the time in Teams." Blinking as if the light hurt his eyes, he stared at her. "You can't carry me as I'm twice your size or more, and I'm weak as a kitten from the damn med they were pumping into me. The docs should have it in the central medicine cabinet. How long before anyone else comes in?"

"Usually no one else enters the area at night, only Matikian and me. I wasn't counting on Peters checking in here again. He may be missed in the other wing because he supervises both areas. If the nurses need him and can't find him—" She grabbed the key cards from the mattress and sprinted to where the meds were kept. It took her precious moments to find the right key and unlock the cabinet. The meds were stored in no order that made sense to her but after shoving containers aside desperately she found adrenaphix injects on a lower shelf and grabbed the entire box. *Thank Thuun I taught myself to read Basic.*

Re-entering Marcus's room, she held out the cartridges and he took one, studied it for a moment before jabbing it into his bicep and grabbed a second. "Civilian dose, practically worthless." He took a third in the other arm.

"Whoa, soldier, go easy on the feelgoods."

Cautiously he straightened, stuffed the remaining injects into his pants pocket and stepped away from the bed. Stretching to work the kinks out of his neck and back, he said, "False energy is better than none. I'll crash at some point so we need to get where we're going."

"I have the key to the rear exterior door to keep the alarm from sounding. This clinic is a few blocks away from my apartment. We—we'll have to figure out what to do from there."

"No groundcar I suppose?" Walking silently on bare feet, he followed her as she headed away from the console, toward the locked rear door.

Carialle shook her head. "Sorry."

Once they were outside in the cool night air and the door whispered shut behind them, he took a deep breath while he checked the immediate surroundings with sharp attention, as if expecting an attack any moment. "I owe you."

"We're not safe yet." She tugged at his elbow and led him in the direction of her apartment building. The street and sidewalks were empty at this hour.

"Your planning is a bit spontaneous," he said as they walked. "But I'm not complaining. It worked. You improvise well."

Carialle looked over her shoulder. *Still way too close to the clinic.* "We're going too slow."

"Doing my best, angel. What did you have in mind to do if I couldn't walk at all?" His steps wavering as if he was drunk, Marcus managed to increase his speed fractionally.

She wished she'd thought of shoes, belatedly realizing the rough pavement must be hurting his bare feet. "The possibility honestly never occurred to me. You have such well-defined muscles, I believed you'd be fine."

He let loose a laugh, rapidly smothered. "Thanks for the compliment but apparently I've been in bed a long time, losing muscle mass and co-ordination. What's the Sectors standard date today?"

She told him and he shook his head. "I can't make the math work right now but probably at least six months. In the military hospital they'd have done therapy to keep my muscles from atrophying. All they wanted at your place was for me to die. No," he corrected himself with a wry smile, "To sign over all my assets and *then* die. How did I end up there anyway?"

"I only know the last part of it but I'll tell you later. We should save our breath for walking."

Eventually they reached her building and she tugged him through the gate with a sigh of relief. Most of the apartments lining the courtyard were dark and she hoped they'd reach hers without being observed. Marcus was leaning on her more and more by the time they finally crossed her threshold. She guided him to the bed, where he sank heavily onto the mattress, head in his hands. After locking the door, she faced him.

"Now what?" They asked each other the question in unison.

Marcus laughed. "Angel, you fly by the seat of your pants, don't you? You had no plan once we got here?"

She shook her head. "This isn't my planet, it's yours. I assumed you'd know who to call for help if I got you out of there. Friends? Distant family members maybe? I expected I'd go my way and you'd go yours." Moving to the kitchen to make tea to calm her nerves, she realized how inadequate her thinking had been. "Are you hungry?"

"I could eat. My stomach probably isn't going to react well at first to real food, just to warn you."

She grabbed a box of crackers and a jar of cingella nut paste and brought both to him. "This usually digests nicely when my stomach is upset, I've found, but the bathroom is through there, if you need to hurl. I'm making tea."

"Got anything stronger?"

"Even if I did, you shouldn't risk it, on top of the meds." She returned to the kitchen area, setting her mug and another equally battered one on the counter for the tea. "A nice hot drink with plenty of sugar will help, trust me."

"Why didn't you call the cops to help me?" he asked. "Instead of doing this risky, hands on rescue mission?"

She gave him a sharp glance, fearing he was being justifiably critical of her efforts but his face was set in an innocent expression and he was busy unscrewing the lid on the jar of paste. *How honest should I be?* Pouring the hot water into the two mugs, she added the tea capsules and said, "I don't have many reasons to trust the cops on any world. And I figured Mrs. Trang probably has friends in a lot of places. I considered making an anonymous complaint but I was afraid she'd kill you before anyone came to check. She has a whole racket going on with disabled veterans at her clinic so even if the police did check on you in response to a tip, she probably could have convinced them you were there under her care legally." She held up her hand to forestall his next comment. "And you wouldn't have been conscious to tell your side."

"I appreciate your taking an interest in my case, believe me. Do they have your home address on file at the clinic?"

"Several people know I live here, in this complex. Why?" She considered his size and added extra sugar to his mug before carrying it to him.

"Sweetheart, when the next staff person walks in and finds those two bastards passed out, me gone and you missing, it won't take the management long to put together the pieces. We can't stay here. We should be on the run now." Despite his declaration of the need to flee, he calmly ate the crackers he'd covered generously with the expensive paste, interspersed with swallows of tea. "I need to eat first, need the energy."

"You don't know anyone to call? No one to come pick you up?" She tried again. One person on the run could escape notice a lot more easily than a couple. He was going to complicate her life even further. "No family?"

"I haven't set foot on this planet since the day I enlisted over twenty years ago. My parents died when I was young and I had no brothers or sisters. I guess the authorities sent me here since it's my home of record, but as far as knowing anyone I'd trust enough to help me right now—" He shook his head.

There was a knock on the door.

Marcus moved faster than she would have thought possible in his debilitated state, grabbing the knife, stepping into her tiny bathroom and sliding the door closed. "See who it is."

She went to the front door and cracked it open. Wrapped in a blue plush robe, fuzzy slippers on her feet, her landlady stood outside. "I need to talk to you." She pushed past Carialle and stood looking into every corner of the room. "Where is he?"

"Who?"

"The boyfriend you snuck in a few moments ago."

"Busted." Phony grin plastered on his face, Marcus emerged from the bathroom. There was no sign of the knife. "Hey, no harm in two consenting adults spending time together. Alone."

"Save it for someone who cares," Mrs. Galaganos said with a frown. "Listen, two sketchy characters were hanging out in the square earlier this evening, asking the vendors about you," she told Carialle. "People I wouldn't want on *my* trail. I don't know what you're mixed up in but you're going to have to run, tonight." Checking Marcus over from head to toe, tsking as she took in his abused, bare feet, she shook her head. "I don't know if he's part of the problem but I want you both gone by dawn, for your own good. And mine."

"Did they come here, to the building?" Carialle's throat was dry and she could barely get the words out.

Mrs. Galaganos shook her head. "The locals know I took you under my wing and they won't betray me, not right away anyhow. I got more than one warning from people I trust. I have friends—everyone knows me and I've done favors for easily fifty percent of the district residents. But money talks and these guys were flashing a lot of credits for any information on finding you. Someone will rat you out, just a matter of time. I'm guessing since you're not at work like you're supposed to be, and we have the company of this unknown, brawny barefoot man, you're in more than one mess. I've heard rumors about the racket Trang runs—enough to know I don't want anything to do with it. I'm guessing he's an escapee. He has the military attitude." She held up a hand. "Don't tell me—the less I know, the better."

Carialle sank onto the bed. She'd known she was going to need to flee, especially after freeing Marcus but suddenly the situation was overwhelming. She was crashing from all the power she'd expended earlier, immersing the two men in deep sleep, which didn't help. And when was the adrenaphix going to wear off in Marcus's body, leaving him to collapse? Would he have withdrawal from the toranquidol? More things to worry about, which pushed her stress level to the maximum.

Marcus continued to make his meal of crackers and tea. "Messes can be gotten out of."

"Well you two are a fine pair, no brains between the two of you." Tapping her foot, the landlady appeared to come to a decision. "Pack whatever you're taking and plan to travel light. I'll only be a minute." She shook her finger at Carialle. "Do *not* leave until I get back."

"We won't." Carialle rose to go to the closet and get out her new pack. Her old pack lay underneath it. She grabbed both.

"Swear." The landlady stared at Marcus. "I want you both off my property but I want the exit to be done right, leaving me in the clear."

"Word of an officer," he said, dusting cracker crumbs off his shirt. "But make it fast."

"Don't need to tell me that." She wrenched the door open and disappeared into the night.

Carialle dumped the contents of the pack on the bed. "Here, you might be able to use this." She handed Marcus the snub nosed blaster she'd taken from Dobkin. "I think it's charged."

He examined the weapon for a moment, clearly at home with blasters, his big hands making the gun appear even smaller and less significant as a deterrent. "An Amarotu Combine special. Accurate, good stopping power, fully charged. Where did you get your hands on an illegal blaster like this?"

She squeezed her eyes shut, trying not to cry. "Please, it's a complicated story and I promise to tell you, but not now, all right? I have to focus on running." Taking a deep breath, she straightened. "You must think I'm stupid, not to have made better plans, not to have thought more than one step ahead. I just—there wasn't much time after I heard what Trang ordered done to you."

He walked over to her, standing close, resting one hand on her shoulder and tipping her chin up with his other, so he could force her to meet his gaze. He was a good foot taller than she. "I think you're gutsy and I admire that. I'll never criticize your planning—I owe you my life and I'm beyond grateful. Any plan accomplishing the goal without casualties is a good plan and you rescued me. Now though, we need new plans. Luckily I'm considered passably proficient at strategy and tactics." He grinned and she felt herself relax into a smile in response. "So tell me, we have the Combine after us?"

"After me," she said, stepping away from his intense regard. "It's not your problem."

"I'm not leaving you alone to deal with the likes of them." His voice was hard.

Carialle shook her head. "You don't need to risk yourself—"

"Besides, Trang is going to want me dead, for fear I'll expose her shady operation," he said persuasively. "So we plot a course together. Where are we exactly, by the way? I didn't recognize the area while we were hiking here."

"South Neridda, in the River Wind district."

Rubbing his chin, he said. "Going to be hard to reach a good place to hide out, on foot."

"There's a mass transit station about a mile from here." She stared at him. "How's your endurance?"

He shrugged as if his condition was of no consequence. "I have a couple of the adrenaphix left."

Mrs. Galaganos knocked and entered without waiting for permission. She dumped a pile of male clothing on the bed and dropped a pair of well-worn but sturdy boots on the floor, throwing a pair of thick gray socks on top of them. "These are my late husband's—he was a pretty tall, husky man with big feet, like you, so hopefully they'll fit. Better than the janitor's uniform you squeezed into."

"The boots are worth their weight in gold to me—I can't thank you enough," Marcus said, comparing one to his foot and nodding. "Barefoot is no good for a soldier."

"I figured as much." She moved closer to Carialle, while digging in the pocket of her blue robe. She brought out a groundcar initiator, brushing a piece of lint off the gleaming surface. "Here, you can't get far enough, fast enough to be safe, on foot or using mass transit. This was my husband's car. I've kept it maintained and fully charged since he died. Even kept the registration current. You'll find it out in the rear parking lot, the blue one with the cherry trim, by the far fence, under a tarp. My advice is to ditch it when you get far enough away. I won't report it stolen for a day or so but one of the neighbors may remember I own it. Lot of nosy people in this district." Impatiently, she extended her hand again. "Well, take the initiator."

"I can't drive."

"I can." Marcus plucked the simple device from the old woman's fingers. "Once I get my situation squared away, I'll have access to my back pay and I'll reimburse you."

Mrs. Galaganos snorted and tossed her head in derision. "I'm keeping her security deposit and I'm sure as seven hells not refunding the unused rent for the balance of the month. I'll also be selling your stuff, so take whatever means most to you."

Carialle gave her landlady a hug. "Thank you for everything. You gave me the first kindness I ever encountered in the Sectors."

Mrs. Galaganos patted her shoulder awkwardly. "I enjoyed having you as a tenant, you made my garden come alive like no one I've ever seen before, you saved my husband's tree...but you have to go, girl. Every minute you delay means either the men hunting you or whatever other trouble you blundered into with him is going to catch up."

"She's right." Marcus grabbed the second hand clothes and headed for the bathroom. "As soon as I've changed, we're leaving, so be ready."

"I don't want to know where you're going. Best not to get in touch with me later either." Mrs. Galaganos disentangled herself from Carialle and walked out the door without a single backward glance.

Galvanized into action, she changed hastily into her most practical utility pants and a shirt. She was already wearing her only pair of sensible shoes. Then she hurried into the kitchen and took her favorite mug and one small birdlike figurine from the collection she'd been amassing so happily since her arrival in the area, adding one new animal done in the cheerful comical local style each week after getting paid. Wrapping the mug and statue in a clean shirt for protection, she tossed a few more clothes in the pack, dodging around Marcus as he exited the bathroom so she could grab a few personal items. A sense of urgency was driving her now, a dread whether the Combine thugs would come bursting through the door, or that her two victims at the clinic would be found prematurely.

"What are you doing?" Marcus came to stand in the door after a few moments. "We need to move."

"I have to get my stash of credits—we're going to need every bit," she said from her perch atop the closed toilet.

"Tell me where it is and I'll do it."

"I can handle it." She pushed aside the ceiling tile and fumbled in the crawlspace above, grabbing onto the pouch where she'd been caching her savings as she accumulated them. No bank for the likes of her. Credits in her hand only. She replaced the tile and gasped as he lifted her down, carrying her into the main room before setting her on the floor.

"We ready?" He tucked the blaster into the back of his waistband, pulling his borrowed shirt out to hide the weapon. "I took a few things, food mostly." He snagged the old pack from the bed. "Let me go first but stay right behind me."

If she hadn't already known he was an elite soldier, she'd have figured it out now, from the way he moved and constantly scanned in all directions for trouble, and the way he consistently shielded her, so any attacker would have to go through him first. They left the apartment complex and paused at the entrance to the gated parking area.

"I see the groundcar, over there," she said, pointing at a vehicle covered with a tarp.

Marcus took her by the elbow and placed her in the darkest shadow, behind a column supporting the roof above. "Stay here until I've got the car running. I'll drive over and pick you up. If anything happens, promise me you'll run and keep running."

His intensity was scary but she couldn't disagree with his order. "I promise."

He left the second pack with her and, blaster in hand, moved fast and low into the parking lot, taking maximum advantage of available cover. Carialle gave up trying to follow his progress and concentrated on getting her breathing and racing pulse under control. She hummed a relaxation chant, dismayed to find the music unhelpful. She was too scared their enemies would suddenly appear in the complex. How long could she hope for, before Peters and Matikian were found? They'd continue to slumber for a few more hours but how long until Mrs. Trang was summoned and a search mounted?

The sound of a revving engine drew her attention back to the parking lot and she hefted the two packs as the groundcar left its spot and came in her direction. The door was opening even before Marcus pulled to a halt and she ran for the car, throwing the packs in the rear seat before she slid into her own place in front with him. He accelerated smoothly and almost ran into the gates as they ponderously slid open. He cleared them with an inch to spare and was driving at high speed away from the apartments.

CHAPTER FOUR

"Should you go so fast?" she asked.

"Probably not but I want to get out of this densely populated area. Too easy to get trapped." He did slow the car's headlong rush a fraction. "Unless things have changed drastically since I left, not many cops in the River Wind district, especially at night." Eyes narrowed, he gave her a sideways glance. "Is lack of police presence why you picked the area to hide in?"

She pondered how best to answer. How much was she going to tell him? "I grew up in such an area on my home world of Tulavarra. I'm familiar with how life runs in a poor district, a slum I think you call it here in the Sectors. So after I esc—once I could look for a safe place, I got on the mass transit and rode until I eventually found River Wind."

"I never heard of Tulavarra before nor have I seen anyone from your planet. Why is the Combine after you?" He made a smooth transition to a wider, busier thoroughfare and sped up again to match the rest of the traffic. Marcus handled the groundcar effortlessly.

"You're an officer in the Special Forces, yes?"

"Well, yeah, retired now, I guess, but what does my rank have to do with anything?" Brow furrowed, he maneuvered in and out of a string of heavy cargo haulers.

"I saw on the trideo you took oaths to defend the Sectors, to uphold the laws—doesn't that make you like a cop?"

"Not exactly. And if you're pulling your information from entertainment trideos, I should warn you a lot of that stuff is crap." He laughed. "I'm just a normal guy with years of specialized military training. And a few classified implants and whatnot I can't discuss." Now he did study her face for a moment before the traffic reclaimed his full attention. "I'm not your enemy, Carialle. I could never be, no matter what's going on. I want to help, if I can. How long have you been in the Sectors?"

"A little over four standard years." She kept her eyes focused on the view out the window, biting her lip. Did she dare trust him? He did owe her a life debt after all, but how much weight did such a thing carry in the Sectors? Marcus kept saying he wanted to help her but she didn't know if she could believe him. The blue flames at his heart said yes but after so much time in the hands of the Combine she was afraid to have hope.

As if sensing her internal debate, he reached out with one hand and captured hers, folding his strong, warm fingers around her fist, giving her a gentle squeeze. "Angel, I think you need a friend and I'm right here, offering to be that person. But if you won't or can't confide in me, I've still got your back."

With a sigh, she turned to meet his eyes and unclenched her hand, twining her fingers with his. "A number of my people were kidnapped from our world by the Shemdylann slavers. We—we had no idea of the realities of the universe until that day, that we lived on a rock orbiting the sun, that there were others—so many others—living in the stars, in the midst of so much evil. Our best weapons were as broken toys against the Shemdylann."

"I can imagine. Rough." A muscle in his jaw twitched, the only sign of his emotion over her traumatic history.

"They sold us to the Amarotu Combine."

"You don't have to tell me any more if it's too stressful. I can color in the rest for myself."

"No, to be clear, we didn't become part of their slave trade and prostitution activity," she said, guessing where his assumptions about her fate had gone. "They wanted us because certain Tulavarrans have a power to influence others, bestowed by our deity Thuun. How did you think I awoke you from your drug addled sleep the other night? Or rendered Matikian and Peters unconscious? Our high priests and priestesses can do such things and more."

"Psychic powers?" He withdrew his hand to adjust a control.

"Of a sort." She missed the comfort of the skin to skin contact with him. Marcus was a very reassuring presence, even debilitated as he was tonight. "The Combine handlers called it empathy. I can see into the soul of a person, read their emotions and desires, and influence them to take action, or to refrain from action."

"Can you kill?"

"I have on several occasions, at my handler's command. I've done many things I'm not proud of. I believe most of the people I killed or influenced against their own best interests were other Combine members—it's amazing to me how violently each group plots against the others at times. But I had no choice on who was a victim and I may well have harmed innocents, to my everlasting shame and regret." Her throat closed with emotion and she bowed her head. Marcus glanced at her but he remained silent.

After a few moments she continued. "The Combine held most of our people as hostages for compliance. If we refused or failed, we had to watch others from our planet die, as penalty for our misdeed." She circled her throat with one hand for a moment. "I was forced to wear a necklace with a bomb inside, so if I rebelled or threatened Dobkin, my assigned handler, he could kill me in an instant. The woman in charge would execute a Tulavarran with a bomb necklace on occasion for no reason at all, as a warning to the rest of us."

Marcus swore a lurid oath. "How did you stay sane through four years of horror? And how did you finally escape?"

"As to sanity, who can say? I had hope. And in the beginning there were quite a few of us together so we encouraged each other." She shrugged. "Over time, hope shriveled as I came to understand the reality and how irretrievably in thrall we were to their evil organization. I was in so deep I saw no way out, yet I was afraid to kill myself."

He reached over to squeeze her hand again. "You're a victim too. You were kidnapped and coerced—"

"I chose to live and my deeds were the price of life," she said, refusing to accept comfort on that point. "Someday I hoped to get revenge, for myself and for the others."

"Understandable. Once we get clear of the current mess, we can work on your situation. There must be a way for you to get immunity in exchange for testifying. I know people in the Sectors I can call for advice."

"Your offer to help makes my heart glad, truly, but I can't involve you in this. Better if I lose myself, as I did for a while in River Wind. I learned much there—I can hide more seamlessly in the next place." Not let herself get drawn into anyone else's problems. But she couldn't have walked away from Marcus. Separating from him at some future point was going to be hard enough. Already his quiet strength and competence, as well as his care of her, were becoming addictive. Not being alone was such a relief.

"A life on the run, working dead end jobs and hiding from the authorities and the mob, is no life. Look, it's decided, I'm helping you get your name cleared and get you resettled in a truly safe location." His jaw was set and his tone brooked no argument.

Carialle could see how he was a leader of warriors.

His interrogation, gentle though it was, continued. "How did you manage to escape on this planet then?"

"When I arrived here to do a job for the local Combine, no one met my handler and me at the spaceport, which was highly unusual. When we eventually found a hotel room, Dobkin got drunk and ingested even more types of other feelgoods than usual, to the point where he passed out, fell, hit his head and died. I freed myself from the restraints, took off the explosive necklace, stole his credits and the blaster and ran. I had nothing to do with his death, but I know how the situation must appear to the authorities. I'm innocent in his case but—"

"I believe you."

"He was immune to my powers, like Mrs. Trang is. The Combine went to great lengths to find handlers with the right genetic quirk."

"But I'm not immune."

She shook her head. "No, you're not. But I'd never hurt you—you're a warrior of Thuun, and those are rare."

"I'm a what?" He laughed again. "I've been called a lot of things but never that."

"Thuun is our god, the source of our power. His highest command states a priestess must always come to the aid of a warrior, or lose her abilities. So when you arrived, I was compelled to act, even though I'm no priestess and you aren't Tulavarran." She studied her clasped hands. "I resisted the call to take direct action at first." It was hard to believe she'd hesitated at all, now she knew more of him as a person. Of *course* he'd needed and deserved her help.

"Hey, it's the result that counts. One thing bothers me though—how many guys did we leave behind? There were a lot of doorways on my hall. How much time do we have to rescue them too?"

She shook her head. "They were already brain dead when I arrived weeks ago. Nothing but the gray mist of the drugs left in their souls. You had the blue fire of Thuun's warrior in yours, and you wanted to live so much—how could I stand aside and let them kill you, soldier of Thuun or not?"

"So how did the Combine find you again, do you know?"

"Dobkin managed to reach one person before he died, Edmorad Zymmer. He was the number four man on Devir Six for a while, so he was well aware of what I could do. Edmorad told Dobkin the SCIA had taken down the mob's leadership in a big raid somewhere and now it was every person for himself. So at least one Combine operative knows I'm here on this planet. I have no Sectors ID so they know I'm trapped on this world. I'm considered a major asset."

And she was probably easy enough to trace, once they got organized to look. Her hair is beautiful with those fernlike green curls but too distinctive—she didn't even try to disguise herself. She has no idea how to play the game she's in. He shook his head. Carialle was lucky to have stayed under the scanners as long as she did. Fortunate for him. Marcus took the offramp to the next major highway, the groundcar accelerating smoothly. The crochety landlady understood how to maintain vehicles at any rate. Once he got his life squared away, he was going to do something nice for her. He and Carialle owed her big time.

Marcus realized his companion was nodding off despite fighting sleep. "Hey, it's fine with me if you want to catch a few winks. We're not being tailed, no immediate danger."

"Where are we going? You seem to have a plan."

He realized she was teasing him a bit.

Lords of Space he liked her. She'd been through a hell of her own and come out strong, and now he'd heard her story he was even more incredulous and grateful she'd risked everything to save his ass. He was nothing to her, all comments about warriors of alien gods aside. "North, to the Gartall Mountains. My grandfather had a cabin in the woods, sitting on a pretty remote parcel of land and I used to go hunting and fishing up there as a kid. Isolated. It belongs to me now of course, haven't been there in two decades, but I never formally transferred the place into my name, so hopefully we can't be traced there. It'll probably be fallen to wrack and ruin by now but it's a safe hideout."

"I can handle roughing it. A forest sounds lovely." She stretched and shifted position in the seat to rest her head against the cushions.

"Are you warm enough?" He set the environmental controls slightly higher.

"I'm fine, thank you. What will we do next, after we reach the cabin?"

He'd been thinking through the issue and had a few ideas. "I'm going to see who's around, who I can get in touch with for reinforcements to get Trang's house of medical horrors shut down. The people I need are probably off planet, so it'll take time. And now that I understand your situation better, I'll work on getting a deal for you." Glancing at her, he took note of the flicker of doubt on her face. He'd have to watch her closely, to make sure she didn't try to run in an effort to save him. He was sure he could save both of them—he just needed a small window of time.

Her yawn was prodigious. "Wake me if you need anything?"

"Of course." He felt like more was required, something to ease her into sleep. What did his mother used to tell him as a kid? "Sweet dreams."

She was asleep in minutes, a shy smile on her face.

He continued to steal glances at her as the miles ticked away on their journey. Shadows under her eyes told him how exhausted and on edge she must have been. She slept all curled up and he wished he could make her more comfortable but the best thing was to get them to the cabin and then figure out a way to work on the next steps. No one was going to make her a prisoner again, not without coming through him. The SCIA or whoever else was doing the anti-Combine work these days would have to accept her innocence based on being a victim herself. Marcus had a lot of back pay banked, which could buy high priced legal help. Carialle risking herself to rescue him had to count in her favor with the authorities as well.

Carialle cried out in her sleep and curled even tighter, as if avoiding a blow. With his free hand he squeezed her shoulder for reassurance. Her tumbled hair was soft against his skin and he forced himself to break the contact. Yeah, she was beautiful and his need to protect her was fierce and instinctive, but now wasn't the time to become infatuated. Or worse.

Might be too late already. The first time he found himself lost in the beauty of her emerald eyes was already one of his most cherished memories.

She needed him to stay frosty, on the edge, combat ready. He was sure the Combine would be after them, with Trang egging them on because he could blow her whole deal. It was only a matter of time.

He frowned as a sudden cramping sensation ran through his gut, followed by a wave of vertigo. A few moments later the pain repeated and his skin began to itch first on his arms, then the sensation spread to his abdomen and his legs.

There was a particularly pernicious itch in the middle of his upper back he was totally unable to reach.

"Fucking hell, did they get me addicted to the junk they were pumping into my veins?" And how bad was the withdrawal and detox going to be? He'd naively hoped all the antivenom and other experimental stuff the military had injected him with over the years would prevent any serious side effects.

He checked the car's chrono to mark when the symptoms began, and estimated how much time they had left to drive. Sure he could set the autodrive function and the groundcar would deliver them to the general area of the cabin, but he had to navigate the old woods road personally and he'd bet a month's pay the track was overgrown and nearly nonexistent by now. His grandfather hadn't welcomed guests other than immediate family so the road was easy to miss. And Carialle couldn't drive under the best conditions, let alone on an unmaintained rural road.

Calling on all his discipline and training, Marcus fought the worsening symptoms for another hour before pulling over at a rest stop, parking in the farthest corner with the groundcar facing out for immediate departure, although there were only a couple of cargo haulers and one camper in the lot. He used half the remaining adrenaphix injects and waited with gritted teeth and clenched fists until the drug kicked in, reducing the worst of the withdrawal symptoms, including the pounding headache he'd developed. He got the car on the road and boosted the speed to the redline.

Carialle didn't wake up, for which he was glad. She didn't need this new worry to add to the stack on her mind.

The adrenaphix began to wear off sooner than he'd hoped, and his physical symptoms worsened. Then the road around him suddenly switched into the empty space in the vicinity of a certain planet where he'd done a hellacious mission. The controls in front of him weren't those of a groundcar but the pilot's readouts for a one man infiltration flyer. "Whoa." Gritting his teeth and operating on sheer muscle memory, he thumbed the car's autopilot on and lifted his hands off the controls. They had an hour or so to travel on the major roads, which the autopilot could handle. But then he had to get them through the dense forest to the cabin. "We'd be sitting ducks stuck out on the main road."

"Did you say something?" Rubbing her eyes, Carialle sat up, although he was only dimly conscious of her presence. "Where are we?"

"About an hour of driving left."

"You're not well—what's happening?" He felt her hand on his arm.

"I'm having withdrawal symptoms from Trang's drug."

"How bad?"

"Pretty fucked. I'm having hallucinations." He hated to admit what subpar shape he was in but she needed to know. "Car's on auto right now, don't worry."

"I'm worried about you." Her voice held a gentle reproach. "Do you have any of the adrenaphix left?"

He closed his eyes tight against the hallucinatory vistas he was seeing. "Pulled over and used up a few earlier. Got two left for when we reach the entrance to the forest."

"You should have awakened me."

"You needed your sleep."

"Stubborn man. Would it help you to sleep now? Until you can use the rest of the meds?"

"I don't know. Why?"

"If the car will drive itself, I can use a touch of my power, put you under, and then awaken you when we reach the appointed spot," she said, looking hesitantly at the control panel.

He stared at her, struggling to concentrate on her face through a mist of overlaid nightmarish visions flickering in and out. "You can send me to sleep?"

"Of course." She gestured at their surroundings. "I see no other traffic, no problems. I can waken you at once if anything changes."

Marcus struggled with his innate reluctance to leave her essentially alone and responsible for standing watch, but he had to admit his control was ragged at the moment, fighting the physical and mental symptoms. "All right, we can try it, but not a deep sleep mind you. Not like you did to those bastards at the clinic."

"Of course not." She scooted over in the seat and set the tips of her fingers on his temple. Her touch was cool, comforting, and a sensation of well-being rippled from the spot where her skin met his. Marcus's eyelids grew heavy and he let his head fall against the cushioned rear of the seat. "Feels good," he murmured.

Carialle withdrew her hand and her power as soon as he was asleep. "Sweet dreams," she said, echoing his earlier good wish for her. Touching him in this condition was painful, as if his skin was harsh sandpaper and she didn't dare go too deep into his aura, which made her nauseous to contemplate. The dead gray of the toranquidol lay over his colors again, the cobalt flames subdued beneath. She wondered if he would be able to throw off the effects of the drug. What a tragedy if they both fought so hard and then he lost the gamble. *I'll do everything in my power to bring him safely through.*

At least the dead black of the alien incursion had gone from his aura, one less battle to fight.

She stared at the landscape they were driving through, the car taking them north at a breathtaking speed. This area was more overgrown than the city and she liked it. She wished she could pull energy from the trees and plants but the car's velocity rendered a draw impossible. *Maybe when we arrive wherever we're going at this mad rate.*

In the next hour she saw no traffic at all, which she found encouraging, and the forest on the verge of the roadway became dense. The vehicle veered into a narrow side road, decelerated and rolled to a halt, the engine shutting off. The sudden silence was deafening. Carialle nudged Marcus. "I think we're here. Well we're somewhere."

He sat up, already fumbling for the remaining adrenaphix injects as he stared a bit vacantly out the windows. "You didn't see anything suspicious?"

"Nothing but a deserted road all the way. We didn't pass any structures."

"Good. Need to stretch your legs or can you hold on till we get to the cabin?"

"How far away are we?"

"Maybe another hour. Depends how bad the private road has gotten in twenty plus years of neglect."

"I'm fine. I'm anxious to be holed up where we can regard ourselves as safe."

"All right then." He jabbed first one and then the other inject into his upper thigh, rubbing the spot absentmindedly. "Oh yeah, the upper helps."

"No more hallucinations?"

"Peripheral. At least I don't itch like I have Denebian sand ants crawling all over my skin right now." He disengaged the auto pilot and initiated the car's engine, driving slowly along the narrow road and peering to the left intently. "Good thing we got here in the late afternoon. Impossible to find this in the dark."

"What are we watching for?"

"A pair of trees, which are probably giants by now, bracketing a boulder resembling a sleeping cat," he said. "My grandfather's private access road was a mile beyond." He flashed a smile. "And the entrance to the road was camouflaged. Gramps was an ex Special Forces guy too, and got a bit intense as he got older."

"You really admired him, didn't you?" she asked, catching the reflection of the familial love in his aura.

"Spent a lot of time with him, up here at the cabin. My Dad was Special Forces too, and gone all the time. My mother was sick a lot." He slowed even further and pointed. "See, there's the rock formation."

If she tried hard, Carialle could perceive the vague appearance of a cat. One sentinel tree stood proud but the other was lightning blasted, its crown broken.

"Now for the road." Marcus sped up briefly and then brought the car to a halt. "Stay here." He jumped out and crossed the cracked pavement, walking along the verge for a moment or two. Striding with his former confidence, he retraced his path to the car and activated the flight capability, bringing the vehicle around in a wide aerial loop and flying about a foot above the overgrown grasses, apparently following a road only he could see.

"I'd couldn't have found this path," she said after a few minutes of their zigzagging between trees and boulders, heading west.

"Even I'm having a bit of trouble. Never dreamed I'd be coming here again, not after Gramps died. And certainly not under these circumstances. We're close now." He set the car onto the surface and drove through a meadow.

Ahead lay a shimmering lake, bordered by more of the towering trees, and a small dwelling nestled in a grove. "It's a beautiful location."

Marcus laughed. "My grandfather cared more about the isolation, the hunting and the fishing than he did for the beauty, but I agree it's easy on the eyes." He parked the car at the side of the cabin and killed the engine. "Let me check out the place first and then I'll signal you."

"All right. I could sit and stare at the forest for hours, so take your time." She reclined her seat and stared at the towering trees through the sunroof. A peaceful lassitude was stealing over her and she knew she'd be able to pull unlimited power from these old growth woods, when she had the chance.

She watched Marcus bound up the steps onto the porch of the cabin and place his hand on a DNA reader beside the door. There was an audible pinging sound and she blinked as a wave of distorted energy flashed over the dwelling and spread outward, dissipating as it went. Meanwhile, the front door obligingly opened. He turned and waved to her so she got out of the car, grabbed the two packs and joined him.

He'd already gone inside for a quick check before hastening to meet her, taking both packs from her hands. "Pretty much like it was when Gramps was here. We put a stasis lock on the whole thing when he died but this is the first time I've been back."

She stepped across the threshold and exclaimed in delight. The interior was undeniably masculine in decoration but appealing, with the wooden floors covered by handmade rugs, rustic paintings on the walls, a couch and chair and shelves loaded with old fashioned books. Blues and browns dominated the color scheme, with a hint of dark green. Caught by a flicker of emotion from her companion, she said, "You miss him, don't you?"

He stood beside the table and touched a pipe resting on a ceramic plate. "Yeah. I almost expect to turn around and see him."

Carialle squeezed his hand in sympathy.

With a visible effort, he straightened. "Bathroom is through there, bedroom on the other side. I'll uh sleep on the couch out here tonight, if you want to go ahead and put your things in the bedroom. I'm going to move the car into the garage."

"There's a garage?" The long gone grandfather had apparently thought of all conceivable aspects when he built the place.

"Well hidden, to the rear. Gramps was thorough." Grinning, he said, "The house AI rebooted when I logged in with my DNA, so there'll be hot water soon if you want a shower. Ladies first."

"And you're sure we're safe here?"

"As safe as we can be anywhere short of being on a Star Guard naval starship. We'll be ok." As he went outside, the AI lit a fire in the huge stone fireplace and Carialle wandered over to watch the flames for a moment. The mix of low and high tech amenities was a bit surprising but she felt at home in the dwelling, welcomed. She gave a quick prayer of thanks to Thuun and asked for a blessing on the spirit of the grandfather who'd made all this possible. The Valerian family might not be of her people but surely there was no harm in requesting a simple blessing. Then she took her pack and his, walked into the bedroom and stopped short at the gigantic bed dominating the space. *Marcus must have inherited his size from his grandfather.*

Setting the two backpacks on a carved wooden chest, she took off her shoes and went to explore the bathroom. A shower sounded appealing.

"I'm back," Marcus called from the main room as she heard the sound of the exterior door closing. "I'm going to see what I can do about dinner, between what I brought from your place and what Gramps left stored in stasis."

"Anything is fine," she said, raising her voice. "And hot water for tea, if possible. I brought tea capsules of various blends, and my favorite mug with me."

"You got it, angel."

Carialle stripped to the skin and stepped into the large shower enclosure, making herself be efficient in the use of water. She remembered her companion was facing more hours of detox and probably wanted a shower even more than she did, after all those days held captive in the hospital bed. Sure, the machines had kept his skin clean but nothing felt as restorative as a shower. Dressing quickly in the spare clothing she'd shoved into the pack, she stacked her other garments neatly folded on the floor. *I can wash them in the lake if worst comes to worst.* Giggling at a vision of herself pounding clothes on rocks like a prehistoric female, she checked her hair and stepped into the main cabin.

Marcus had been bent over the closest chair, clutching the top rail with his fists, but at the sound of her arrival, he straightened and smiled. The cheerful expression clearly cost him to maintain. "Food's ready."

Going to him, she looked closely at his face and the pain lines bracketing his blue eyes. "You're not doing too well, are you? How can I help?"

"I'll be all right. You should eat." He hastened into the kitchen and dished up two plates of beans and noodles in a delicious-smelling sauce. Juggling the plates, he also brought her a mug full of steaming water.

"Give me a minute!" She made a dash for the tea capsules in her pack and then joined him at the table, where he'd politely waited for her.

Carialle ate with good appetite but noticed he hardly touched his meal. "I'll clean up, since you cooked. Why don't you get that shower now?"

"I won't argue, thanks." As he rose from his chair, he staggered ever so slightly. "By the way, the cabin is surrounded by sensors a mile out, so no one is going to sneak up on us unannounced. And the windows and doors are locked and blast proof. We're safe."

For now. She bit her lip but kept her pessimism to herself. "Thank you for telling me. So your grandfather liked living in a fortress apparently."

"You don't know the half of it."

She stretched and tried to unkink the tense knots in her back from the earlier events of the night. "Well I for one approve. It's nice not to be scared and at risk for a change."

He entered the bathroom, shutting the door as he did so. A moment later she heard the water cascading in the shower. Carialle finished the few dishes before strolling to the front door so she could gaze at the forest beyond. Being here in the midst of so much wild nature was feeding her energy levels to some extent, but she couldn't wait to access the planet's power via direct contact with the ancient trees, whose roots would run deep. She wished she'd asked Marcus if she could venture outside for a few moments before dark fell. *I wouldn't mind explaining the mechanism of my abilities to him.* The ex-soldier was a good listener and their situation required mutual trust.

The water was still running, she realized. Concerned, she went to knock on the bathroom door. Hesitating for a long moment, she decided better to be overcautious. The withdrawal symptoms were clearly overtaking him again. "Marcus? Are you doing all right?"

Chapter Five

There was no answer. She slid the door aside and gasped as she saw him slumped in the shower, on the floor as if he'd slid down the wall like a broken doll, head tilted against the wall. Despite the hot water, he was shivering and she could tell from a faint odor in the air, he'd thrown up earlier. Rushing in, she turned off the water and grabbed the large towel he'd laid on the counter. "Can you stand? Marcus?"

Dazed, he couldn't focus his attention on her, blinking and barely conscious so she stepped into the enclosure and wrapped the towel around him as best she could before urging him to his feet. "Lean on me."

The shudders racking his body threatened to topple her along with him as she got him moving in the direction of the bedroom. He collapsed onto the bed and curled up in the fetal position, moaning. He moved his hands over his arms and legs, scratching at himself. She was afraid he'd draw blood if he kept it up.

"I'll go see if we have any adrenaphix left," she said.

He shot out his hand as she spun on her heel and held her with a grip of iron. "This is going to be bad," he said between gritted teeth, each word enunciated as if his life depended on it. "Help me get dressed and make it outside. Can't risk being in here with you. Might hurt you."

Shocked, she sent a wave of soothing power at him and tried to uncurl his fingers, knowing she was going to have bruises but unsightly contusions were the least of her concerns. "You won't hurt me and I'm not going to put you outside to suffer through this alone like a dying animal. Don't be absurd."

"Stubborn angel," he said, slurring the words. "I'm going to be sick again."

She grabbed the nearest receptacle, an ornamental ceramic bowl, and held it for him, rubbing his shoulders with her free hand while he suffered an attack of the dry heaves. "I'm going to get you the clothes, so you'll be warmer," she told him when he lay back, exhausted. "But no more talk of going outside. We'll deal with one problem at a time and be fine."

"Should be something in the closet." He gestured vaguely at the far wall.

She grabbed a faded pair of sweat pants and a soft knit shirt from a shelf in the alcove and with a lot of effort managed to get him into them.

"Burning up," he said.

Checking his forehead with her hand, she was shocked to find his skin now hot to the touch. At least he'd stopped scratching his arms.

"I'll be right back." Carialle walked into the main area of the cabin, leaving the bedroom door open and took a deep breath. Her insides churned and anxiety threatened to choke her breath off. She had to regain her self-control or Marcus was right and they'd never get through the night. "Treat each symptom as it presents," she admonished herself, taking a deep breath and holding it. "He's strong, he wants to live, he'll get through this." Part of her problem was sheer terror that he might indeed die as the drug left his system. *I'm not a priestess—I can't heal him.* She turned as he groaned loudly and called her name. She needed to keep him well hydrated, not only because he was vomiting and sweating, but also to help wash the remaining poison from his system. Quickly she made more tea, adding plenty of sugar and took the mug plus a tall glass of water into the bedroom.

"Can you sit up enough to drink?"

With her help, he scooted against the carved headboard as she hastily piled pillows behind him. He drank the tea in a few gulps, followed by the plain tap water and then fell on the massed pillows, eyes closed. "Having hallucinations again, and an assortment of really bad thoughts," he said in a weary voice, as if the act of talking was almost more than he could manage. "If you won't let me out of the cabin, then you should tie me down, in case I get violent."

Tears in her eyes, she climbed onto the bed. The idea of restraining him even for her own good was too much like what had been done to him at Trang's clinic. And to her by the Combine. "Roll onto your stomach and I'll rub your back," she offered. "I have soothing lotion—it might help the itching."

Obediently and in slow motion he moved onto his stomach, pillowing his head on his arms, watching her. "Carialle, I can kill you with a single blow. If the withdrawal takes me out of my right mind, I might—"

"You won't hurt me." Patiently she folded his T shirt up to his shoulders and massaged the lotion into his skin, while sending him supportive energy. "I'm sure."

"Smells good," he said a moment later. "You rubbed some on me at the clinic, didn't you?"

"On your poor wrists, yes. I'm sorry it's so floral."

"S'all right. The sweet scent is how I knew you were real, not a dream. Gave me hope."

He drifted into restless sleep for a few minutes and she was encouraged, but then he moaned and convulsed. She scrambled off the bed and stood helplessly, watching him arch his spine and writhe. Taking a deep breath, she tried to shut out her own worries and took a deep look at his aura. The gray no longer ate at the edges of his blue flames, but twined through the center like snakes or ropes, as if trying to separate the blaze into smaller segments. Attempting to make the fires representing the core of who he was as a man easier to destroy? Make him easier to kill? She sent her own strength to feed the blue flames, launching dark purple birdlike avatars to swoop onto the gray tendrils, clawing and biting and tearing them to shreds. If he couldn't defend himself, she'd do it.

How long their battle lasted she had no idea but the gray retreated eventually so she opened her eyes. Out the window across the room she could see the moon had risen so hours must have passed. *No wonder I can hardly move.* Marcus lay crosswise on the bed, breathing heavily and covered with a sheen of sweat. Carialle trudged to the bathroom to make cold wet compresses and then bathed his forehead, arms and chest with the refreshingly cool towels.

He sat upright with an energy he hadn't displayed all evening, startling her into dropping the wet towel and backing up a step. He held one hand as if he wielded a blaster and his eyes narrowed as he surveyed the room, presumably searching for enemies. "Quick, get behind me so I can protect you."

"Marcus, it's all right, there's nothing here, no one but us."

"The Mawreg and the Chimmer are coming—I can hear them."

His voice was hoarse and he gestured with his free hand. "Hurry up and get on the ship before they surround us."

This is really bad. Unsure how to reach him in his hallucinatory state, she crawled onto the mattress and worked her way behind him, looping her arms around his waist to make their contact closer. Again she examined his aura and was dismayed by the darkness of the gray intruding on his soul. She summoned her energies and visualized a sword, chopping through the mass of gray, dicing it up into smaller and smaller particles, which her swooping purple avians could consume. The gray sent writhing tentacles at her, trying to suck her into its maw of nothingness but she kept her weapon moving at a blinding speed, fending off such attempts. Through her battle, Marcus muttered and shook and tore at his own skin, first blazingly hot against her body, then shivering cold. As she finished destroying the last of the visible gray, he cried out and collapsed against her.

Carialle laid him flat and wriggled aside. Shaking with exhaustion and fear, she slid a pillow under his head, pulled up the heavy quilt and got off the bed. *Time for brewing more tea, while he's unconscious or sleeping.*

Running to the kitchen, she made a mugful for herself and one for him, and refilled the water glass. Leaning on the counter, she pushed her loose hair wearily away from her eyes. For a healing this major there should be a lead priestess and several secondary priests or priestesses, as well as body servants to help with the physical tasks of keeping the warrior comfortable. Not one incompletely trained woman all by herself, battling the evil to save the warrior and trying to keep his body alive at the same time.

And I am no priestess.

Despairing as she heard him stir in the other room, she wiped away tears. *He needs me to survive but he has no idea what a weak reed he's leaning on.*

You have the power, you were born with it. The quiet voice speaking in her head sounded like the wind rushing or the ocean waves crashing onto a beach and she pulled upright in shock.

Nothing else was said, but a wave of cool energy ran through her body, head to toe. Her fingers and toes tingled with the sensation. When she exhaled, her first breath was frosty, visible in the dimly lit cabin. Goose bumps ran over her skin, subsiding a moment later. *Could Thuun have reached to touch me with his power?*

Marcus called her name and she returned to the battle for his life.

Carialle had once heard it said the darkest hours were those before the dawn and now she understood, for her warrior's body began to fail, his heart beating erratically, and still she had to fight the gray, which continued to encroach on his blue flames, as it withdrew from his mind and body, making a last stand to claim him and kill him.

She held him close, his head pillowed on her breasts, and tried not to be distracted by worry over his infrequent breathing, as she sang her defiant chant over and over. Holding him tight, she refused to surrender. From the few words he uttered sporadically, he was seeing enemy aliens surrounding them and believed he was doing his best to fight to protect them both. What scared her was she too was beginning to see flickers of alien beings herself, as she inserted herself deeply into the fray, as she used her resources and power to battle the evil swamping him and keep his heart beating. Was she going to die if he did?

Probably.

Marcus's arms tightened his embrace. "Not going to let them have you," he said, although it was unclear what enemy he was referring to. "Die to protect you."

She sensed the loosening of the bonds between worlds, life and death mingling in the room, each trying to claim them.

Now what? She whispered a desperate prayer to Thuun, begging for inspiration, a new strategy to try. *Hear my plea, help me again.*

Taking three deep breaths, she sat up straight and sang the ballad for a new dawn, new beginnings. It wasn't viewed as a battle hymn, or even a particularly religious song, being left over from an earlier, more primitive time when it was believed priestesses had to sing to coax the huge Tulavarran sun into the sky each day, pulling it over the horizon with chains of harmony. Few even knew all the words any more but it had been a favorite of hers as a child. The music was glorious, full throated and resonant with power and she gave it her all, reaching deep into herself for the last untapped reserves. Extra power came to her from some unknown source, potent in its ferocity, protective. The water glass shattered as she hit a high note and she felt Marcus's blue flames blazing higher and higher, as they hadn't done for hours, being nearly embers a moment before. Maybe he'd received a portion of the unknown burst of power as well. Whether her warrior intended it or not, he was giving her what she needed, his renewed will to fight to live on in this world, not slide into death. She hit the penultimate note, held it and then topped it with the final note, at which point the sun would have risen on her home world.

Eerie mists swirled in the room, lit with purple and blue fires. Marcus sagged against her, but breathing steadily. She checked his aura and to her relief found no more gray, not even a fleck.

Panting, Carialle slumped against the headboard, no strength left in her body.

She smelled a faint sweet burning smell, accented with a hint of vanilla or perhaps cherries, and saw a man's shape at the door, not a real man but the outline of one.

"Well done," he said, before walking away. The eerie colored mists drifted out of the room after him, as if drawn by his energy.

"Gramps," Marcus murmured, stretching slightly and turning on his side with a yawn.

Or Thuun. Carialle laid her hand on his forehead, relieved to find his skin a normal temperature. Tears of sheer exhaustion rolled down her face. The battle was over. She and Marcus had won. Thuun himself and who knew what other resources had come to their aid in that last desperate hour, but her warrior would live.

Morning sun warm on his face woke him and Marcus rolled onto his back, opening his eyes and studying the roughhewn planks of the cabin's ceiling. Cautiously at first and then with more energy, he did his isometric muscles, testing each major group of sinew and fiber and finding himself strong, without aches or pains. His mind was clear and sharp, no hint of the drug's stupor. And no hint of the tainted residue the Mawreg prison had left on his soul. He possessed jumbled memories of the last twenty four hours—a montage of Mawreg and other aliens, him driving a groundcar, pain, danger, wild colors mixing in the air like spilled antigrav paint—but mostly what he remembered with no difficulty was Carialle. Her touch, her songs, her fierce determination—all those threads wove through his memory and he understood he owed her his life twice over now.

Sitting up, he looked at the rumpled bed and wondered where she was. He threw off the heavy quilt and got up. He heard Carialle singing outside and his heart beat faster with impatience and longing to see her. Walking barefoot toward the main cabin, he stubbed a toe on a small obstacle and bent to retrieve his grandfather's pipe. Unsure what the memento was doing in the bedroom doorway, on the floor, he made a side trip to replace it on the table, inhaling the scented and spicy aroma of Gramps' special tobacco mix. *Who'd have imagined the scent would linger all these years?*

The front door was open and he shook his head ruefully at Carialle's complete lack of situational awareness. *Lucky she has me.* There would be no more moments where she had to take on the burden of defending them. Defense as well as offense if needed was his job and as he was returned to full strength, he intended to fulfill his obligation.

As he stepped barefoot onto the porch, he halted in sheer amazement, speculating with unaccustomed whimsy whether he'd gone through a portal to another world. A thick carpet of riotous multicolored flowers bloomed overnight between the cabin and the lake, with large iridescent flying insects of a type he'd never seen before gathering nectar. Carialle was standing at the edge of the water, one hand palm down on the bark of a huge tree beside her, and she was singing the most beautiful song he'd ever heard. The melody was unearthly and sublime and her voice did full justice to the ripples and trills of the complicated score. Above her a flock of virtually every kind of bird on the planet swirled, singing along with their own music, augmenting the joy of hers. As he waded through the knee high flowers, he caught glimpses of various shy woodland creatures at the edges of the meadow, watching Carialle sing. Even his presence didn't scare them off, for which he was glad.

I feel like I wandered into a fantasy trideo.

Her voice was the golden thread tying the incredible experience together and his heart beat faster as he walked closer. She was facing the lake but as if sensing his approach, she did a graceful pivot for the last few notes and sang them directly to him.

There was a moment of silence after she finished and then the birds arrowed over the lake in a broad swath of colors, breaking apart into flocks of their individual species and flying in different directions.

"Well?" she said, head tilted.

"I should be applauding but then again, the song was so amazing, mere applause would be an insult." He reached her side and without pausing to think it through, gathered her close in his arms and kissed her.

For a moment she stood in his embrace as if surprised and then her lips parted, inviting him to deepen the caress. She put one hand on the back of his head to hold him in position and leaned against him, her softness cushioning the rapidly growing hardness of his body.

Her mouth was hot, sensual, and tasted of her sweet tea. Exploring her with his tongue, he felt all the nerve endings in his body going on the alert, tingling with desire. Marcus picked her up effortlessly and she twined her legs around his waist.

He ended the kiss, breathing hard. Carialle laid her head on his chest and the soft green tendrils of her hair tickled his chin.

"I—I'm sorry," he said, setting her on her own feet and steadying her on the broken ground for a moment. "You—the song—"

She shook her head, taking his hand and leading him along the lake shore to a large flat rock, dappled with bright green moss. "Don't be sorry. I'm not. Emotion between us runs high, especially after last night's battle." Carialle sat, patting the gray surface beside her in invitation.

Marcus put himself right next to her, not wanting to lose the physical contact. Knowing she was holding him through the night had been a lifeline. Here, in the daylight, health restored, his emotions were running hot along more sensual lines. Everything about her fed his desire.

"No need to ask if you feel better today." Laughing, she gave him a saucy glance, allowing her gaze to linger for a moment on the bulge in his sweat pants before she picked up a few pebbles, and tried skipping one across the surface of the lake.

"Like a new man. Or like the old me, before my last combat mission and certainly before Trang go her claws into me." He took her hand and turned so he could see her face. "I don't know how to thank you for sticking with me last night. For saving my life again. I can't truly recall all the details but I know I nearly died. Except for you, I wouldn't be sitting here. I don't know how a man repays such a debt." He looked closely at her. "Are you all right? You didn't get any sleep."

"I'm fine, full of energy." She waved her hand at the trees surrounding them. "This forest has deep roots and gave generously of power this morning. I'm restored to myself as well. It's been a long time since I was in a place where I could drink deep of what I need, could tap the energy of a living planet. Devir Six, where we were based, is mostly desert, and on my other Combine assignments offworld I had no opportunity to do more than sip."

"You consume energy? But I've seen you eat food." He was confused but intrigued.

"I eat to maintain my physical body, like you. Although I probably eat a lot less than you do." She gave him a playful elbow jab in the ribs. "But for my power, I need to draw upon other sources. Calling upon nature for energy is the gift of Thuun to his priestesses. For their part, the priestesses nurture living things, perform healing—" She broke off and frowned. "The polar opposite of what the Combine forced me to do."

"I remember you telling me you weren't a priestess. But you have the powers of one?" He sensed from her demeanor and expression this was an important subject for her.

"You gave me a gift last night, Marcus Valerian," she said, formality ringing in her tone, as if she was a queen addressing a knight. "One I had no slightest expectation or hope of ever receiving."

"I don't remember. I remember doing a lot of puking, hallucinating—" He was embarrassed at how much he'd put her through but grateful beyond words she'd hung in there with him.

"On our planet, the gifts of Thuun come to men and women in certain family lines," she said. "Only they can become priests and priestesses."

"But you have the powers—I've sure seen the evidence myself. How are you not a priestess?"

"My father was from one of the noble houses. My mother was a servant and of course after she got pregnant, she was cast out. I was raised in an area like River Wind."

"A slum," he said.

She nodded. "But since I was born with the power, my mother told me I'd be a priestess, filled my head with talk of how carefree my life would be. And hers, by extension, as the mother of a priestess."

"A lot of pressure to lay on a little kid," he said.

"She was trying to give us both hope. At the age of eight, which is when training begins, she took me in my best clothes to the temple one morning, to enter the school. I was turned away. The priest was contemptuous. He said even if I did have a measure of the gift, I'd be an embarrassment to the family my father was from. Too many questions would be asked. We fled home in disgrace and never spoke of the temple again. My mother died within a year. I believe the crushing of her dream of a better life for us was too much for her heart to bear."

"Did your father help you?"

"No. I never spoke to him in my entire life, although I knew who he was and I saw him fighting the enemy, defending the temple on the day we were kidnapped by the Shemdylann. He died a valiant death."

Marcus put an arm over her shoulders and hugged her. "I'm sorry. So how did you survive?"

"After my mother died, I marched to the temple and told the priest since Thuun gave me the power, I had to be allowed to serve."

"You were what, nine?"

"Yes, and desperate. Without my mother to protect me, the slum was a dangerous place. Certain men pay well for young girls."

"Those men don't deserve to live." Anger at what she'd endured rose hot in him. He wished he could have been there to stand for her.

"Thuun maintains a special level of hell for them, or so the accounts say. Which doesn't help their victims much in life, and I was determined not to become prey for such a one." Carialle shrugged. "The priest—a different man than the one who'd rejected my application away the year before—chose to be amused at my impertinence and said of course I could serve the temple, as a maid."

"You were a child." His protest was immediate and again he wished he'd been there to help, although he'd have been only a few years older than she was at the time. He marveled at what a caring person she was, despite the rigors of her childhood.

"I didn't care what working conditions he set. A job—even cleaning the least appealing of the temple's many chambers—was an honest way to live. I got myself a safe home, enough food, decent clothes. I was inside the gates, you know?" Eyebrows raised, Carialle shot him a smile showing her satisfaction at the betterment of her situation she'd achieved so young. "I cleaned and I ignored the taunts and bullying from the high born girls who could be priestesses. I had nothing to do with the boys destined to be priests—avoiding them was the safest course. The temple had a huge library and I'd sneak out of my bed in the servants' dormitory at night and disappear into the stacks. My mother'd taught me to read so I was able to glean quite a bit from the volumes in the library. Several of the elderly celebrants were also willing to tutor me on the sly if I brought them extra food or cleaned their rooms with attention to detail. So I have gaps in my knowledge and learning, but I can wield my power."

She watched the waves on the lake for a few moments and he was reluctant to break her mood with questions. "It's ironic, but after I was kidnapped, the Combine ranked me as one of their best assets among the Tulavarra. Not that I was any more compliant than the others, but because of my power. There were two sisters, priestesses from the southern continent, who were kind to me, taught me what they could while we were in captivity together. Not at all like the haughty girls where I grew up. I could have been a priestess had I been born where those two lived, my birth no barrier. But we have to take the portion we're given." Carialle straightened and turned to him. "Do you know what is required of each applicant before becoming fully vested as a priestess or a priest?"

He shook his head. "I can't imagine."

"Man or woman, each must overcome a challenge. It's a ceremony known as Thuun's *rukauntir*—his required proof of worthiness. Usually it's an arranged challenge—a wilderness journey alone to retrieve a hidden treasure for example, but the test can also be a real life experience, like serving in the midst of an epidemic, protecting one's self and healing a certain number of people. I wouldn't have been given a chance at *rukauntir* because of my birth." Carialle patted his arm. "Until you. Our struggle last night was my *rukauntir*. I heard the voice of Thuun at the darkest moment and I took heed, reached deep inside me and found what I needed, with your help."

He gathered her close, his intention primarily to offer comfort but he admitted to himself he craved skin to skin contact with her again. She felt so right in his arms. "And we survived."

Carialle wiped away a few tears with the hem of her shirt. "The warrior and the priestess," she said.

"A good team." Being part of the team was the foundation of the Special Forces. He'd expected to miss that the most once he was involuntarily retired but Carialle had all the guts and smarts a man could ask for in a partner. Overwhelmed with unaccustomed emotions, he tilted her chin and kissed her softly on the lips again.

She allowed her tongue to trace the seam of his lips and when he parted to give her what she sought, she shifted herself onto his lap. His arousal had to be blatantly obvious to her at this point, pressing into her bottom. Carialle was beautiful, warm and delicious and he wanted to carry her inside the cabin and spend hours making leisurely love to her. He put one hand on her breast, cupping the soft weight through the fabric of her shirt, and her sigh of pleasure as he rubbed the pebbling nipple went straight to his cock. "I want you," he said, breaking off the kiss and nuzzling the delectable spot where her neck met her shoulders. He wished he had more elegant words but his desire for her was overwhelming his verbal skills. "We could go up to the cabin." Kissing his way up the slender column of her neck, he nibbled her ear lobe. "Sound like a good idea to you, my lovely angel?"

"I have a better one." She slipped from his lap and stood in front of him out of arm's reach. Slowly she removed her shirt, revealing lacy blush-colored underwear accenting the allure of her ample breasts, lifted and ready for his attention. Carialle's cheeks took on a pink tint under the pale jade of her skin as she watched him, took in his hungry attention to her figure. "I treated myself to something pretty with my first week's pay. I wasn't exactly expecting to display my body to anyone—I simply wanted to please myself." Her tone betrayed a flicker of nerves.

"The view pleases me, no argument there. Gorgeous." He reached for her but she danced out of his way with a graceful sidestep.

Holding up a finger in a mock chiding gesture belied by the smile on her lips, she said, "Not yet." Now she shimmied out of her utility pants and revealed another bit of lacy lingerie perfectly designed to tempt him while not concealing anything. Swaying her hips, she returned to his arms and yanked at the hem of his shirt. "Now you."

"You've seen me—I'm nothing special. Even my scars and tatts are gone, thanks to the rejuve the military doctors ran me through." He yanked off the T shirt and allowed her to lower his sweat pants, freeing him. Cool as the morning air was, it did nothing to decrease his ardor or the size of his painfully throbbing erection.

She eased the pants off his ankles and tossed them aside. Remaining on her knees before him, she ran her hands up his thighs, leisurely caressing the muscles, and then cupped his balls for a moment before stroking his erection with a firm grip. Her sensuous touch had him fighting not to come in response to her skillful ministrations. "I don't count the times I glimpsed your body, my warrior, for those were without your permission and under duress. This is the view I wanted—you as a free man, desiring me."

He ran his hands through her hair, enjoying the tactile feel of the unusual curls, and traced the delicate shell like forms of her ears with his fingertips. "Desire isn't a problem—my self-control is. I'm right on the edge here. You're the most desirable woman I've ever seen and the only thing I want right now is you, splayed underneath me, taking all I have to give."

Her hands on him were driving him crazy and he wasn't going to last long, despite his fervent intentions. Groaning, he pulled her from her knees and onto his lap, his cock jutting between them, hot and hard, weeping with desire. She adjusted herself, rising to allow the tip of his arousal to touch her soft inner folds. Using one hand, she directed him into the soft, slick channel, while she held his body close to hers with the other hand looped behind his neck. Her lush breasts pressed against his chest. Marcus held her tight as she lowered herself, taking him slowly, inch by inch, allowing herself to grow accustomed to his girth.

"I knew you were built like a warrior all over but the reality is overwhelming," she whispered, pausing.

He held absolutely still, barely breathing, although he wanted to seat himself deep inside her body for their mutual pleasure. "I'm not hurting you, am I?"

Carialle shook her head. "I'm no untried maid, but it has been a long time since I held a man and never one such as you."

Marcus found he hated the idea of any other man experiencing this closeness with her, but he couldn't change the past, for either of them. *No man but me going forward.* On the undeniably possessive thought, his hips pumped automatically and she cried out, clutching him tight as he plunged deeper into her. Her inner muscles clenched around him and she threw her head back, moaning low sounds of pleasure challenging his control. Carialle did something with her hips that applied insanely erotic pressure on his shaft, lodged deep in her most secret places. Holding her so close he was afraid she wouldn't be able to breathe, he pumped harder and felt himself release, the pleasure so intense he nearly blacked out. A moment later she matched him, screaming his name into the forest silence as she climaxed, and then leaned into him, sweaty, limp and sated.

He nuzzled her neck, relishing the unexpectedly tender feelings rising in his heart. "That was amazing but over too fast. There are so many more things I want to do with you when I've recovered a bit. We need to get to bed, where we can enjoy each other properly."

Carialle ran her hands over his chest, touching his nipples, tracing the muscles of his abdomen as her hand drifted to where they were still joined. "Do you not like the bed I've prepared, my warrior?"

Marcus didn't understand her meaning until he took notice of his surrounding while calculating how he'd carry her to the cabin. While he'd been distracted, emerald green moss had grown in a lush carpet encircling the rock where they'd been sitting. Holding her, he rose to his feet and stepped away, going a few feet into the moss, surprised at how soft and thick the surface was. Surely there were stones and tree roots underneath but he found none of those poking through. Carefully he laid her on the woodland mattress, after checking one-handed to ensure there'd be nothing to hurt her there.

She lay staring up at him with those luminous green-and-golden eyes, fingers of one hand lightly resting against his chest. "So my efforts please you after all?"

"After the last few days, I shouldn't be surprised by anything you do," he said. "You're a constant amazement."

"You did tell me we were alone here," she reached up to pull him on top of her for a passionate kiss.

After a moment, he rolled onto his side, facing her, using one hand to fondle the tempting breast before lowering his head and taking the still pebbled nipple into his mouth. Carialle arched under him, murmuring her approval of his attentions and slid her own hand down his body to caress his balls and the highly sensitive area behind them. After a few moments, he switched his attention to her other side, trying to ignore the skillful way her hands were encouraging his cock to stand at attention for the next round.

"Please," she said, "I want you inside."

"I can't deny you anything, angel." He positioned himself between her thighs and guided himself into her softly cushioned channel again, the sensations heightened this second time by the sensual memory of their incredible first encounter. She locked her ankles, holding him tightly in place as his hips pumped and he thrust with all his power.

He captured her hands, holding them above her head, cushioned by moss, as she moved together with him in perfect harmony. He kissed his way up the graceful arch of her neck, capturing her lips for a deep kiss leaving them both breathless until the moment his climax triggered hers and there was only the intensity of their mutual passion.

CHAPTER SIX

Carialle lay under her warrior, her body warm and satisfied, tingling with the aftereffects of their lovemaking. She held him as tightly as she could, craving the connection and the shared emotion. He rolled off her and onto his side, but kept his hand on her hip, not breaking the contact. She'd drawn on the energy of nature to enhance their passion, and fed back the beauty of the moment to the world surrounding them, as she'd never done with any other man, and the exultation and pleasure had been mind blowing. For him too, she hoped. She was glad he'd accepted her offer of a moss-soft bed, under the trees, for their first real coupling.

As if reading her mind, Marcus looped her hair behind her ear, leaned over to brush a kiss on her lips and said, "That was the best experience of my life."

Carialle shivered as a breeze touched her. "I think I'd be willing to adjourn to the bed now though."

Marcus laughed. "Yeah, kinda drafty out here, although I didn't notice before. Pillows are good too."

He helped her to her feet and gathered up their clothing. He handed her the lacy bra with an awkwardly endearing bow and said, "Now I know you enjoy sexy lingerie, I'll be buying you more."

Her cheeks grew warm as she blushed uncontrollably. "We can discuss my underwear later."

"Anything you want." Marcus swept her into his arms and carried her effortlessly up the hillside to the cabin.

Devotion to Carialle's pleasure was his theme the rest of the afternoon as well, exerting himself to find out what aroused her and shattered her self-control the most. Carialle knew herself to be less experienced than her warrior, but she rapidly came to a few discoveries of her own as to what it took to bring Marcus to the edge and hold him there, before they went crashing over in unison, to their mutual delight.

Taking a break for a leisurely meal they cooked together in the small kitchen and consuming the simple food in bed, sharing one plate, feeding each other, laughing at each other's jokes, snuggling beneath the covers, secure in the isolated cabin, Carialle felt as if her life had literally turned upside down. No longer a lonely, hopeless prisoner, she experienced a giddy happiness at finding this sturdy warrior to stand at her side, be her friend.

The last time they made love, Marcus holding her close as she wrapped herself around him, bodies moving in perfect unison, she sought to enhance the moment even further, peeking at the colors in his aura, sure she'd find the bright red of true love.

Shock nearly paralyzed her for a moment and she forgot to breathe. The red strands were there but subdued, held in abeyance by the blue flame, as if he was fighting the emotion even as he bedded her. Her own aura would show the orange of pain and the muddy browns of confusion now, and instinctively she pulled back with her powers.

"Hey, you're thinking way too hard," he said, nipping at her shoulder and then kissing her neck as he toyed with one nipple, rolling it between his fingers. "If you're too tired—"

"Not at all," she said, disengaging and moving to where she could take his steel hard cock into her mouth, pleasuring him with her tongue and hands to avoid having to converse while she was uncertain. There was definitely love there in his heart for her, but just as undeniably, he wasn't entering into the bond wholeheartedly and the hesitance made her sad. *I'll fight for his heart...*

He knew he'd done or said something wrong but he had no idea what. Carialle withdrew emotionally from him in an undefinable fashion during the final moments of their lovemaking. She drifted off to sleep and he tucked her in before pulling on his pants and heading into the main cabin to check whether his grandfather's coms room was operable.

When she'd slept enough and rejoined him in the kitchen hours later, she was her usual cheerful self outwardly, but he sensed a reserve in her manner.

"I'm making dinner," he said, immediately feeling like an idiot because it was obvious what he was doing as he flipped the meat he was grilling. Being tongue tied in her presence hadn't been a challenge before, but the knowledge something was out of kilter between them made him awkward.

"I think the smell is what woke me up, so delicious." She took a seat at the table and played with his grandfather's pipe. "How was your afternoon?"

"Happy to report I made progress." He brought two plates to the table and made a second trip for her mug of tea. Dropping a kiss on her cheek as he presented the drink to her, he studied her face for a moment, realizing her smile wasn't quite as happy as usual. Not his imagination—there was a problem.

"You're staring," she said, filling her spoon with savory stew. "Oh, this is so delicious."

Dissatisfied but unsure how to ask a question, or even what the question would consist of, he sat across from her and dug into his own meal. "I threw together a bit of everything in the stasis stores. Gramps was prepared for a siege, or wintering over maybe, so I had good ingredients to work from. Nothing ever goes bad in stasis."

She waved her hand at the rustic cabin. "How can you be making progress on finding us allies? I love it here but there does appear to be a lack of what I've come to recognize in the Sectors as modern communications."

Rising, he held out his hand, "I'll show you."

She set her spoon on the saucer and joined him. He guided her to the center of the room, knelt and moved the carpet, revealing an antigrav platform. As soon as they'd stepped into the plate, he tapped his toe on a small black spot on the edge, nearly invisible, and the platform sank into the floor. She clung to him as they descended inside a shiny antigrav tube and the platform stopped in a brilliantly lit corridor below ground.

"I don't dislike antigrav as much as I hate cryosleep," she said, "But it's not my favorite way to travel."

"Hang onto me and you'll enjoy it, I promise." He knew he was grinning. "In fact, sex in antigrav has its own interesting aspects—"

"I think we've arrived," she said, stepping away.

Her reaction wasn't quite what he'd expected, given her earlier enthusiasm in the bedroom. Before he could ask a question, she strolled to the first door. "What did you bring me here to show me?"

Relieved to have a topic to talk about other than emotions and relationships, which weren't his strength, Marcus escorted her down the hall, which ran under the cabin, naming the doors as he proceeded. "Weapons room, storage room, communications room." He ushered her into the latter and made a grand gesture at the bank of coms units on the far wall. A single chair sat in front of the controls. "The tech is old now of course but it was top of the line in Gramps' day, and I've been out in the interstellar chatter, searching for certain old friends who can help me."

Carialle advanced into the room, trailing her hand along the elaborate display. "You did warn me he was intense."

"Yeah, we Special Forces guys have a tendency to compensate in other ways when we retire. We're used to having the best intel, weapons and coms and we don't take well to being cut off once we leave active duty. He didn't spend his pension or his credits on anything else, my grandmother being long gone, so this cabin and outfitting it properly was his hobby. And acquiring his armament, cached in the weapons room. I can show you the armory later."

"I probably won't appreciate the no-doubt deadly contents enough to please you, but I'll be glad we have them if the Combine unexpectedly catches up to us." She sat in the chair, spinning in it like a carefree kid. "So what did you learn? Who have you talked to?"

"I lurked for the first few hours, had the cabin's AI do a bit of general investigating for me, then I hacked into a few places. The AI is outdated too but learns fast and Gramps programmed it to be as stubborn and dogged as he was. This scheme of Trang's and the doc heading up the veterans' bureau here on the planet is ugly and much bigger than you and I thought. I found out she has ten of those clinics, scattered between the capital city and elsewhere."

Eyes wide, Carialle said, "You're not serious? How many people has she murdered in those places, I wonder?"

"Hard to tell. A big percentage of her business is legit, an actual medical urgent care and rehab practice. So maybe not as many as you and I are afraid of. But it tells me again how lucky I was to end up in the one where you worked." He squeezed her shoulder.

Blushing, she blinked. "Have you found any old friends who can help?"

"I figured I needed to get the lay of the land first, especially since I'm not sure how I ended up on Felicia Seven, and who was involved in faking the paperwork to send me to Trang's place. Gotta be sure who I can trust before approaching anyone directly. I'll work on it more tonight."

"Peters told me someone was asking questions about you," she said, with the air of a person suddenly remembering a critical point. "I'm sorry—I completely forgot in all the stress of the rescue. The inquiries were the trigger for Trang's decision to speed up your injection doses."

"While that's helpful to know, even if you'd told me before I detoxed, it probably wouldn't have sunk in so don't be too hard on yourself."

Carialle sighed as she ate her breakfast the next morning. Last night had been awkward, the two of them lying in the big bed spooned together. There was a silence between them that hadn't existed before, as if there was so much to say but neither wanted to risk asking the wrong question. She wanted so much more from him than the physical aspect of his body pleasuring hers, wonderful though the lovemaking had been. Why would he fight the deeper feelings? Maybe a tough soldier didn't know how to let himself be in love. What did she know of warriors, after all? Only legends, and those invariably spoke of the warrior and the priestess as a couple, lacking any details of how the relationship developed. She watched him moving in the kitchen, cooking his own breakfast now, whistling a tune slightly off key.

He brought his plate and mug of steaming coffee to the table and sat, but made no move to eat, finally exhaling and reaching across the table to take her hand. "Carialle."

Startled, unable to read the meaning behind his serious tone of voice, she looked him full in the face. "What's the matter?"

"Yeah, my question exactly. I was going to give this problem time, see if I could figure out the answer myself but I gotta hit this head on. Life is too short for guessing games."

"You're confusing me."

"I'm confusing *you*? That's a good one." A muscle twitched in his clenched jaw. She'd never seen his demeanor so serious. "Yesterday morning, in the woods and in the cabin, we were good together, astoundingly in sync. I never had such an intense level of connection with a woman before and the sex was mind blowing because we were so emotionally involved. There's a bond between us after what we shared together the night before—don't deny that. Then all of the sudden it was like you withdrew and I'm going insane trying to figure out what I did or said to upset you, or hurt you. Whatever it is, I will fix it, I will make up for it, I will swear on my life not to do it again, but you gotta tell me where I went wrong. I'm not psychic, angel. I refuse to lose you because I can't read your mind. I'm falling in love with you, damn it." Marcus swallowed hard and glanced away for a moment before he turned his gaze back to her face. "I never said those words to a woman before, not ever."

She realized she had to explain, she'd been wrong not to ask him questions when she first observed the mix of emotions stirring in his soul. Trust lay between them. She had to rely on the bond forged in the fire of *rukauntir*. "Your colors, your aura scared and saddened me."

His hand tightened on hers. "My what?"

"You know I told you I see people's souls, for lack of a better word, and I know what they're feeling. The gift of Thuun is empathy."

"Empathy on hyperdrive," he said. "What's that got to do with us?"

"I took a look at your aura, when we were in bed yesterday and I saw the beautiful red tendrils of true love—"

He nodded. "Damn straight, glad you could read me. So where's the problem?"

"You—you were resisting the emotion. You didn't want to feel love for me." Tears trickled down her cheeks and she brushed them away impatiently. "And the realization broke my heart. Because I love you." She studied his face. His eyes were narrowed, and his forehead was furrowed. The set of his shoulders was tense as he rose from his chair and came to her side of the table. He drew her to her feet and stood close, holding her in his arms. She laid her head on his chest and took comfort from the steady beat of his heart.

"Don't read my goddamn aura right now," he said, rubbing her back in slow circles, his lips close to her ear. "Listen to my words. When we were making love, I was going crazy with concern and desire for you, with the urge to protect you and keep you safe forever." He raised one hand as she opened her mouth to speak. "Hear me out. We have a saying in the Sectors, 'if you love something, set it free. If it returns it's yours. If not, it was never meant to be.' I believe we're meant to be but you've been a prisoner for the last four years. Even after you escaped, you were living life on the run, looking over your shoulder every second. I told myself maybe I needed to give you space, to have time to find out what freedom would be like, to find your way, to see if I'm really a man you could love, or if this—this passion between us was a result of all the adrenaline and the circumstances and because I was helping you escape. I didn't want my love to be a prison you fell into because of gratitude, okay? So I worried maybe I should go slower on the relationship and because the idea hurt like fucking hell, yeah I was probably all roiled up in my damn colors but it doesn't mean I don't love you." His voice rose. "I'd lay down my life for you, right now, and all I want is your happiness. I didn't want to rush you into a commitment you might regret later."

Stunned by his intensity and the undeniable truth ringing in his voice, Carialle was silent.

"I probably never said so many words at one time to any woman in my entire life. So if you're going to rip my heart out, because the damn colors were wrong, go ahead. I don't do auras, I do words, maybe not well but I gave you all I have."

"Please—" She curled her fingers around his. "I never thought I'd be lucky enough to find you," she began in a halting voice she didn't recognize as her own.

"Yeah, I know, I'm the warrior who gave you your chance at razzmatazz or whatever it is. I helped you get your promotion to priestess." His voice was low and bitter. "I want to be more."

"*Rukauntir* and yes you did facilitate my trial, without meaning to do so. The warrior and the priestess are one of the oldest stories in all of Tulavarran lore and do you know what the source of their power is, according to legend?"

"I was paying attention—your god Thuun." He shifted his feet as if preparing to disengage and move away. "This isn't getting us anywhere."

"The warrior and the priestess share the truest love, the most unbreakable bond," she said, tightening her grip to hold him in place and make him listen. "It's their gift from Thuun. Words are your way, the empathy is mine. May I show you what's in my heart? Will you let me prove to you I need no time to reflect, no time to doubt the genuine nature of my love for you? I know my heart and it's yours. I'm not in love with you because you saved my life. I'm in love with you because you *are* my life, from this point on."

Now he did stare at her, his blue eyes blazing. "I'm not a psychic—how can I see anything?"

"Trust me to share." Praying to Thuun, she sang a song, one of the oldest, the chant for the binding of a warrior and his priestess. She reached for his other hand and brought their clasped hands to her chest while the words and music tore from her throat. She sent her power flying, pulling her deepest emotions and tugging at his. A moment later they were surrounded by a mist of lavender, cobalt blue and vivid red, as if they weren't standing in a cozy cabin, but had reached a magical destination, just the two of them. He tugged his hands free but only to pull her close in a tight hug. Carialle held out her hand, palm up, and a swirl of blue, shot through with the pure red, settled onto her skin. "Your heart," she said. Now the vision was joined by another swirl, lavender, also laced intricately with the red. "My heart."

The colors flowed into each other, drawing each other closer, until there was no way to tell where each one began or ended. The colors exploded into a shower of multicolored sparks, whirling in the air, around Carialle and Marcus for a moment, as she felt an indescribable sensation at her core—warm and sensuous, bringing her to tears. She hoped and prayed he experienced the same reaction.

Marcus captured her lips in a deep and demanding kiss, taking possession of her with intensity that left her breathless. He made his claim on her with everything he was and she answered in kind.

The sparks of their love continued to dance over them for a moment longer and then winked out.

"We're bonded," she said. "There's no need to set me free and I'll never go away. I love you."

He leaned his forehead on hers. "Promise me if there's ever any more doubt in your mind, you'll talk to me, no matter what the colors tell you."

"I promise."

The rest of the morning was spent most agreeably in the bedroom, followed by a quick lunch.

"I'd better get back to the coms," he said as they cleared the remnants of the meal off the table together. He reached for her. "Although I'd rather do other things—"

She danced away. "Save the thought for the evening. I should go outside and draw more energy from the forest. There's no telling what might happen when we leave the cabin eventually—I'll need to have full reserves of power available to me."

"Don't wander too far."

"Nothing in the forest can harm me," she said in surprise.

"Humor me. I'm probably being overcautious but I don't like you out there alone." He raised a hand to stop her protest. "I'm not doubting your abilities, for which I have huge respect, but if anyone does find our trail and follows us up here, I want us to be fighting them together. We're stronger together."

"I can understand the logic." The reminder they weren't entirely safe in their isolated location put a small damper on her mood. After giving him a kiss, she left the cabin, ran downhill to the edge of the lake and stood staring over the sparking blue water. Carialle considered the epic nature of their time together so far. Freeing Marcus from the clinic, their long drive north to the cabin and then the battle to survive his detox had all been adrenaline-filled, high stakes events, followed by mind blowing sex. Now was the time for them to get to know each other in more depth and build on the foundation the shared danger had provided. Carialle laughed quietly to herself. She was a priestess after all, one who nurtured. Surely she could nurture this relationship that meant so much to her, especially now they'd realized how necessary it was to talk things over, for her not to rely solely on her empathic gifts where Marcus was concerned. *Stronger together indeed.*

She strolled along the bank, pausing for a moment to admire a raft of scarlet water lilies blooming close by in the lake. The absence of the ever-present, colorfully winged insects customarily sipping nectar from the blooms seemed odd. Raising her head to listen, she realized the woods were silent this morning, no bird calls.

Retreating a few feet inland, she selected one of the largest trees and laid both hands on its trunk, seeking the flow of energies circulating in the woodland.

Intruders.

Shocked, she gasped and recoiled. *I have to warn Marcus.* The newcomers alarming the wildlife and birds could only be Combine. Somehow the tenacious enemy had tracked her here. Maybe the ownership of this place wasn't as well buried in the records as Marcus believed. There were no other cabins and the whole area was posted against trespassing, he'd told her, so the arrivals were unlikely to be innocent tourists or campers. She took off running, working her way through the trees, seeking a more direct path to the cabin, frustrated by dense thickets of thorny berry bushes and stands of close-packed saplings.

Moving more silently than the forest creatures, Marcus met her half way, with a lethal, heavy duty blaster in hand. She was out of breath from her exertions and before she could say anything, he'd tackled her and dragged her behind a huge tree, kissing her as he did so. "Scared me to death not knowing where you were. I was terrified those bastards had gotten to you." He drew her behind him and cautiously reconnoitered the forest beyond the cabin, in the direction of the road.

"You know company's coming, right?" she whispered.

Jaw set in a grim line, he nodded as he quartered the surrounding area, seeking signs of their enemies. "Sensors were triggered and my first priority was getting to you before the bad guys did."

"Give it up, folks, and we'll make this simple," said a voice from concealment ahead and to the left of them. A blaster bolt hit the tree well above their heads, making Carialle duck as bark flew and Marcus covered her.

"You're trespassing—get off my land," Marcus shouted.

"We're way past worrying about petty crimes, soldier. Give us the girl and we'll kill you ourselves, a clean headshot, right here, right now, no more of Trang's drug shit."

Marcus fired the blaster and Carialle heard a yell, choked off. He held a finger to his lips and then flashed two fingers at her, pointing to the right. She placed one hand on the tree, seeking to gain information on where exactly the intruders might be.

Screeching, a flock of birds burst into the sky and Marcus fired again in that general direction. Several bolts came blasting through the branches, uncomfortably close to their position.

"We want the girl alive, asshole. She belongs to us and you're messing with more than you understand. Quit trying to play the hero—you're outnumbered." This was a new speaker. "Make me mad and I'll hand you over to Trang myself and watch while she tortures you."

"We're pinned down," Marcus whispered. "I killed one and winged another. Don't know how many more. We've got to get to the cabin."

Carialle whispered a quiet acknowledgment and set her other hand on the tree, trying to impose her will on this one and its fellows. Marcus bracing her with one arm provided comfort and support but all her concentration was for the interaction with the sentients embodied in the trees.

There was a deafening cracking sound, as if lightning had struck nearby, and the ground shook, followed by a cloud of dust billowing through the area. Screams echoed. Carialle grabbed his hand, stepped away from the tree and broke into a run.

Marcus was right on her heels. "What the seven hells happened?"

"I convinced one of the sister trees to drop a decaying branch above their hiding place. The trees say more men and vehicles are coming." As she spoke, she heard the growl of engines for herself, not too far away.

Cursing, Marcus picked her up with one arm and broke into a sprint with speed she couldn't have matched. He zigzagged a bit on the hillside path, as if avoiding enemy fire, but bounded straight up the stairs of the cabin and made it through the door as twin blaster bolts struck the roof support, the porch collapsing right behind them, splinters flying. Still holding her, Marcus slapped the controls inside, next to the door. "Full defenses," he yelled. "Scanners up."

There was a hum and the AI reported. "Engaged."

The cabin shook as an explosive round detonated on the roof, blocked by the building's faltering shields.

"Grab our stuff, we're leaving now," he said, moving to the scanners, focus switching from one to the next, calculating odds. "At least fifteen men, with heavy duty weapons. They're not kidding around."

Carialle forced her leg muscles to engage. She sprinted to the bedroom and grabbed their two packs, taking a moment to veer into the kitchen and retrieve her mug. As she passed the table, she took Gramps's pipe and stuffed it into her pack as well. "Ready," she said, already kneeling to shove the rug aside, uncover the gravlift and activate the mechanism. There couldn't be anywhere else Marcus expected to go, not with the cabin surrounded by Combine thugs. "Hurry."

He retreated from the door to join her and as the platform sank with nerve wracking slowness, she realized he was saying a final farewell to the cabin which held so many of his best boyhood memories.

"Plan?" she said. "Won't we be trapped here? I mean, they'll get in eventually."

"You don't know the half of how paranoid and prepared my grandfather was. Although clearly the old man should have installed more sensors, further out. I'll rectify the oversight, if I ever have the chance." He secured the blaster in his waistband and jumped off the platform before it finished its journey. Above them the cabin rocked as another barrage hit it. He held out his arms in invitation and without hesitation she stepped off the edge of the gravlift and fell, to be caught in his rock hard embrace and set on the floor.

Marcus was already moving to the coms room.

"Calling for help?" she asked, following in his wake. "Will anyone arrive in time?"

"The cabin has a self-destruct mechanism. Setting it to blow when the attackers breach the door. Debris will cover the entrance to this area, but we won't be here in any case."

She touched his arm. "I'm sorry."

"For what?" He didn't look at her but ran past her to the weapons room and grabbed an assortment of heavy duty blasters, handing her one.

"Costing you your cabin," she said as he rejoined her.

He leaned over to kiss her even as he was closing her fingers on the gun. "Losing the cabin is worth it to me—I'll sacrifice whatever it takes to keep you alive and safe. We can rebuild. Now stay close."

Marcus jogged to the storeroom, which she'd never been in, and opened the portal, motioning for her to precede him. The door shut hard behind them as more dust rained down from the one sided battle going on above. Marcus opened a small safe with his palm and extracted various credit tags and other objects, handing them to her to dump into the pack. She heard him give a grunt of surprise but couldn't tell which of the items falling into the pack had elicited the surprised reaction. Then he pivoted to yank a shelving unit on the rear wall away from its position and Carialle gaped as a narrow tunnel was revealed.

"Take this." He handed her a handlamp, already switched on. "Hurry, I'm guessing the defenses are about to crash under the assault and we gotta be far away from here before then."

Drawing a deep breath – she wasn't claustrophobic but the dark, musty-smelling tunnel was uninviting – she ran headlong. She heard his footsteps pounding behind her and the ambient light cut off, so she guessed the entrance was sealed. "How far?" she asked over her shoulder.

"The tunnel runs about a half a mile."

"I'm having trouble breathing." Pausing in alarm, she pressed one hand to the center of her chest.

"Air down here must not be circulating. Better keep walking, angel. I can carry you but once I pass out, we're done for." He squeezed her shoulder. "Give me the packs."

"No, you have all those heavy weapons. I'll be fine." Breathing deep from her diaphragm as singers were trained to do brought a bit of relief. She told herself there was enough air here for them to get wherever they were going. To believe anything else would be self-defeating. *Trust Marcus.*

The ground shuddered and the tunnel floor tilted under her feet with the shockwave. Marcus grabbed her and ran to the next bend, debris falling like lethal rain behind him. He barely cleared the section of the passageway they'd been in when the whole thing collapsed, sending choking dust into the air. Carrying her, the packs and the weapons, showing no signs of fatigue or physical distress, Marcus forged ahead.

"Not far now," he said in between coughing spells.

"That was the cabin blowing up?"

"Probably."

"So the thugs'll think we're dead and stop hunting us." The idea made her happy.

"Can you walk?"

"Sure."

He set her down and they continued on their way. "This bunch is determined to recapture you," he said. "Clearly I'm incidental to them."

"Miscalculation on their part."

Flashing a grin to acknowledge her flattery, he said, "We're not clear yet but we are at the end of the tunnel."

Looming in the glare from the lights was a blank wall.

He set his hand on a reader off to the side and the portal slid up over their heads, folding itself neatly. Marcus drew her forward and then closed the odd door again. She stood in a small space, next to a mini ground car facing toward a ramp leading upward.

"Let me check the situation outside." He set the packs next to the car and squeezed past the vehicle before scrambling up the ramp. A moment later he said, "Can you get into the car?"

"Sure, but is it going to start after twenty years sitting here?" Carialle was dubious but worked her way into the passenger seat. There was hardly any room between the car and the wall.

"I hope so. Didn't see any bad guys out there—this is another back road emptying onto the main road south of where we drove in to reach the cabin."

After squeezing himself into the driver's side, he sat behind the controls and reached for the initiator. "Say a prayer or hum a chant or whatever's most suited to encouraging a cranky old engine."

"Actually my gifts don't work on machines at all," she said with an apologetic smile.

"Encourage me then."

The engine fired up immediately, with a hum of power Carialle f ound reassuring.

Marcus gave her a fleeting look. "We're going full throttle in case anyone is waiting to ambush us. Get low in your seat and hang on."

The ground car shot forward so fast she was pressed against the cushions as she crouched in the foot well. They left the concealed garage in an instant and were speeding down a road as overgrown as the one leading into the cabin had been. Jaw clenched, Marcus drove around and above obstacles with consummate skill and hit the two lane road in a few heart stopping moments, accelerating to the south. She admired his skill and yet again took relief in the fact he was willing to help her.

"Anyone behind us?" he asked.

Trying to control her pounding pulse rate, she checked. "No, we're clear."

"It'll take them awhile to figure out we're not in the cabin. The way it was built to collapse if the self-destruct was ever activated, the ruins should have fallen in on the underground rooms, which will also help to hide the fact we had a chance to escape. But if and when they run a scan for bodies, it'll be obvious we got away somehow."

"Intense is too mild a word for your grandfather," she said, facing forward in her seat again. "I would ask why he planned for such extreme situations but considering his precaution saved our lives, I can't be anything but grateful. Where are we going now?"

"Actually, back to the city. I found out a few helpful things this morning before we were attacked." Frowning, he checked her over. "You sure you're all right?"

Yes, I'm fine, not so much as a scratch. We aren't seeking shelter at my apartment are we?"

"Lords of Space, no. Showing our faces in River Wind would be asking to get taken. I have a safer place in mind, now I've gotten my hands on ID and credits again, thanks to Gramps. In a major stroke of luck, I think I may have found out who was asking awkward questions about my disappearance."

Since he didn't seem upset by this development, she hazarded a guess. "A person you can trust?"

"With my life and more importantly with your life," he said. "My battle buddy Sam Garamonte. We grew up together here on this planet, enlisted together, survived Hell Week together in the Teams, and served together on several missions I can't talk about. I lost track of him when I got assigned to a highly classified task force in the outer Sectors and he deployed elsewhere. Our careers went in different directions, different theaters of the war. Come to find out he took early retirement for medical reasons a couple of years ago and he's here, on Felicia Seven. You'll like him."

"Should we involve an innocent civilian in our problems though?"

Marcus smothered a laugh. "Innocent? Can't remember the last time Sam was accused of being innocent. Wait till you meet him. He's as intense as Gramps was, as I am. The best part—he's a high ranking cop now. He's the perfect person to involve. I bet he had something to do with me getting assigned here for rehab. Team guys tend to stick together—we have an unofficial network Command doesn't sanction but highly effective nonetheless. He'd have heard I was busted up badly. He owes me for pulling his sorry ass out of a few firefights in our early deployments, so I could see him trying to keep track of me. He'd know I had no family left."

"Sam sounds better all the time." She craned her neck to verify whether they were still in the clear. "No pursuit. I guess we fooled them pretty well, at least enough to buy time to escape."

"We'll be on the main freeway soon. Less chance of an attack there."

"Are you sure you can trust this man? If he's been on the planet a few years—" Carialle was afraid to get her hopes up. She'd overheard too many Combine conversations about crooked cops on the payroll during her missions with Dobkin.

"I'm positive. But I'm not going to risk you. I've got a plan for taking this in stages. Keeping you safe is my highest priority."

CHAPTER SEVEN

Carialle's nerves spun up as the car entered the outskirts of the city. Her blood pressure rose, her heart pounded and waves of nausea swept over her. Taking herself into the Combine's territory was terrifying. Judging by the massive attack on the cabin, the Felicia Seven branch of the crime organization had restored itself efficiently and in force. She glanced at Marcus and bit her lip. He'd protect her with his life but she didn't want things to come to that, so she hoped he was right he had a safe place for them to hide, and his friend would be able to assist.

Marcus drove into a high end district close to the spaceport and pulled into the sweeping driveway of one of the top hotels on the planet.

"What are you doing? We don't belong here." She spread her hands, gesturing at her dusty, torn top and utility pants. "The management will throw us out."

"Well, I'm sure there'll be raised eyebrows at my antique groundcar, but the staff of the Baredjim Interplanetary Suites knows better than to take anyone at face value. A generational billionaire can wear tattered clothing and drive a heap. My credit balance will speak for me. I accessed accounts Gramps had hidden and let's just say we couldn't stay here forever but we can afford a week or so."

"Even I've heard of them - Baredjim is the most expensive hotel chain in the Sectors, right?"

"Angel, not only can we afford it, thanks to my grandfather's generosity, we're taking one of the best suites in the house." He handed her out of the groundcar and then retrieved their two packs. The human valet took the car away without a blink.

Marcus escorted her into the lobby, despite her qualms. She stood silently while he registered them, and clung to his arm as the gravlift carried her aloft by his side. As soon as the door closed behind them and they were alone in the gorgeous suite with an eagle eye view of the city, he tossed the packs onto the gold and white couch and drew her close for a kiss.

"I could use a bath—how about you? The desk clerk told me there's a hot tub big enough for us to share," he said teasingly. "We're both covered in dust from the tunnel collapse."

She ran her fingers through his hair, enjoying the feel of the heavy strands, so unlike her own. "Please, tell me why we're here?"

"Fair enough. Part of what makes this place so expensive is their guarantee no guest will have his or her security compromised. The place has AI's, highly trained security forces, even D'nvannae Brothers on staff to ensure no one is bothered in any way within these walls. Team guys go to work for Baredjim on occasion, handling security detail after they retire from the service. Top notch organization." He drew her into the bedroom as he talked and sat on the end of the massive bed, positioning her between his knees. "I'm not risking you by taking you to the first meeting with my old friend. I need a lot of written assurances about your safety and status as a victim before I take you anywhere the SCIA could get their hands on you. I'd like to talk to a lawyer first as well. But I can't leave you anywhere the Combine can easily access you while I'm gone." He waved his hand. "This place is a fortress, and I'll have as much peace of mind as I'm going to get when I'm not by your side to defend you myself." He scanned her face. "Is the idea okay with you? You seem uncomfortable—you're supposed to talk to me when you have doubts, remember?"

"We used to stay at hotels for the most part when we traveled on Combine assignments. Hotels don't have good associations for me, not even ones as high end as this one."

"I never thought about that." Frowning, he glanced at the room as if seeing its appointments for the first time. "I was strictly operating from a need to have you stashed somewhere relatively safe. I can't see Sam until tomorrow morning—he's out of coms reach—and when I do go to his office, I won't be able to concentrate if I'm not sure I left you in a safe place." He studied her expression. "We tried hiding at a remote, isolated location and look how that worked out."

"And I regret the loss of the cabin," she said. "But we did have two precious days of freedom there."

"Yes, we did. I'm sure once I've seen Sam face to face and gotten assurances about your status we'll be moved to a safe house while events settle out. So you won't be here long."

"Leave me a blaster," she said, forcing herself to smile since Marcus was so concerned about her being happy with the arrangements he'd made. "I have my powers but there are five percent of humans I can't affect, according to the Combine. Blasters work on everyone, right?"

"Energy weapons kill the good and the bad just as easily," he said.

"All right then." She freed herself from his embrace and took one of his hands. "I believe you mentioned a bath?"

Hand in hand they wandered into the huge bathroom together and she exclaimed over the gigantic tub. "It's like a small pond."

"Warmer, with less seaweed and no curious fish," he said with a laugh. "Shall we take a dip before dinner?"

"Absolutely."

They undressed each other with much laughter, kissing and intimate touches while the tub filled with water set to a mutually agreeable temperature. The bath lasted so long Marcus had to ask the AI to refresh the water twice to keep it from going too cold. Eventually he wrapped her in a huge, fluffy blue towel with the hotel's crest and adjourned to the bed.

Much later, after a room service dinner containing many courses because Marcus insisted she try a bite of numerous delicacies, they went to bed and cuddled while the AI ran a trideo newsfeed.

"Nothing about the cabin," Marcus said finally, flicking the control to shut off the programming. "Or us. I wondered if Mrs. Trang might have filed a police complaint."

"The Combine works in the shadows."

"Was she Combine?" he asked. "You never mentioned that."

"I don't know for sure, but anyone running an operation like hers would have to be connected to some degree." Based on her four years' worth of hard won knowledge on how the syndicate worked, Carialle had no doubt. "She'd rather get them to wipe us out quietly and hope to preserve her clinics."

"Which isn't going to happen, not after I get done talking to Sam tomorrow." Gently Marcus shifted her aside, putting her against the pillows before he slid off the bed. "There's something I need to give you."

"A gift? When did you have time to buy me a present in all our crazy adventures?" She clasped her arms over her knees. "It's not my birthday. Is there a major Sectors holiday I should know about?"

He gave the pack a scowl. "This thing is getting ratty and way too dusty to be on the bed with us."

"Not to mention it was Dobkin's." Carialle repressed a shudder.

"Even more reason to get rid of it." He picked the old backpack up from the floor and set it on the table beside the windows. "To address your question, I didn't buy anything and no, this isn't a holiday." He dug through the contents, searching for whatever he intended to give her.

When he turned, he had a small wooden box in his hand and his expression as he walked toward the bed was anxious. "I hope you'll like it."

"I'm sure I'll love it." She resisted the urge to read his aura.

Pausing next to the bed, he said, "It's fine with me if you want to check my colors. I don't want you to ever stop being yourself—I love you exactly the way you are. I just wanted you to promise to *talk* to me if you're ever unsure about me or us."

"I remember." She smiled and sent a tendril of her power to see what his mood was—happy but anxious apparently.

He sat on the bed. "Hold out your hand."

She did as he requested and he put the now open box into her palm. Juggling it a bit, she gasped. "How beautiful!" The box held a ring, with a large white stone in the center, flanked by two diamonds on either side. Carialle had never seen anything like the center stone before, with coruscating flashes of blue, green and red color under the milky surface. As she tilted the box this way and that, different colors dominated. "Stunning—the red is the exact color of our love."

Marcus took the box from her hand and removed the ring, setting the container aside. "This was my grandmother's. The stone is an opal, from Old Earth. My family was First Ship on Felicia Seven and the legend is the ring belonged to the actual Felicia, brought with her from Earth on the colony vessel, and passed down over the generations."

"First Ship? Like nobility?"

He laughed. "Maybe on more status-conscious planets. Means my ancestors were among the crew of the first ship to claim and colonize this planet. The captain was my many times great grandfather, as a matter of fact, so he had the privilege of naming the star. Although it has a long scientific name as well." He studied the ring for a moment. "I believed this was gone, lost maybe when my grandmother died, but then I uncovered the box in Gramps's safe when we were evacuating this morning. I know he'd want you to have it."

"I'd be honored to wear it." The ring appealed to her as no other piece of jewelry ever had. The colors entranced her and seemed so perfect, both in terms of who and what she was—a seer of colors—and as a symbol of their relationship as well. She held out her hand.

Marcus took it and she was astonished to feel a slight tremor in his. "Carialle, will you marry me? I know I'm rushing things," he said before she could utter a syllable, "But after what we said to each other today, I want to make sure you never have doubts of me ever again. I want to give you all the reassurance you need."

She stroked his cheek with her hand and leaned forward to kiss him on the lips. "You worry too much, my warrior. No one can break the link between us. I have no need of rings or outward symbols, although I very much want to marry you."

"That's a yes, then?"

Carialle nodded.

With a whoop he hugged her and then slid the ring on her left hand, where it fit perfectly.

"I do have a gift, of sorts, for you," she said, when the long and involved kiss that followed his putting the ring on her finger ended. She left the bed to grab her pack, opening it while he watched in puzzled silence. "Close your eyes."

Obediently he did as she asked and held out his hand. She placed the pipe across his palm and closed his fingers on the stem. "I saved this for you today."

She observed a hint of moisture in his eyes as he examined the pipe. "Gramps was never without it—thank you, angel."

"I—I thought we saw him, the night we fought through the *rukauntir* together. You said his name at the end. There was a scent in the air, a whiff of something—the smoke from this perhaps? I know we had help from outside of ourselves and I assumed it was Thuun. I know it was Thuun for me but perhaps the shade of your grandfather came for you as well." Carialle debated for a moment and said, "I gave you another gift as well. At least I hope it was a gift."

Head tilted, Marcus raised one eyebrow. "I don't remember. If it was when I was out of it—"

"It was when you were first brought to the clinic. Before I knew I had to rescue you." She drew him to sit next to her on the bed. "I hope I did the right thing."

"I'm sure anything you did for me in Trang's hellhole was right." He put one arm around her shoulders and gave her a hug. "Tell me."

"Most of the time when the toranquidol was wearing off, you'd raise a fuss, demanding to be set free."

He nodded. "I remember. If I ever meet the bastard in charge of the injects again, he's a dead man."

"I saw how he treated you. The way he talked and acted was unforgivable."

"A sadistic, petty tyrant, who took pleasure in the fact I couldn't get loose to defend myself. Yeah, Mrs. Trang hired some real pieces of work. My fiancée excepted." Smiling, he kissed her forehead.

"Other times you'd go into rages, fighting the restraints and convinced you were imprisoned by the Mawreg," she said.

"Yeah." Color rising in his cheeks showed how embarrassed the admission made him. Jaw clenched, a muscle twitching in his cheek, Marcus focused on the far wall instead of her. "Lotta guys have problems after combat, flashbacks and whatnot, it's pretty common."

"And you have those issues, like any other warrior who's seen terrible things and done what he had to do to defend his people," she said. "No shame there, no judgment, my love. But this was different."

"Different how?"

"I believe the Mawreg infused something into you, so deep you didn't consciously know it was there. Neither did your military doctors." She spread her hands and fumbled for the explanation. "I'd never seen anything like it. Three pools of oily, dead black and underneath the surface there were colors I have no name for, morphing and moving and trying to spread into the rest of you, take you over perhaps."

Marcus sprang to his feet and paced. "Are you saying the enemy planted a parasite? Because I'm getting fucking unnerved here, I won't deny it."

"Not a physical parasite as you'd define it, no. But your captors left something anchored in your mind."

"I was positive something was wrong with me after I was rescued, I *knew* it, but no one would listen." He slammed his fisted hand against the palm of the other. "I felt it." He swung around to stare at her. "You shouldn't be near me—we don't have any idea what those alien bastards might have planted in my head. I won't risk hurting you."

She left the bed and went to him, forcing him to accept her hug. "No, listen to me. You were fighting it, battling hard. Your mind had constructed barriers enclosing the implants and you were trying to destroy them. I simply added my own power to the fight."

His arms were holding her like bands of steel. "Tell me you succeeded. Tell me I'm not contaminated or a time bomb or...or I don't know what."

She framed Marcus's face with her hands and pulled his head down until she was nose to nose with him. "The black is gone, I give you my word before Thuun, this is the truth."

He searched her face for a long moment. "I trust you. Why didn't you tell me before?"

"Because there were more pressing issues facing us, especially since the implants were destroyed."

"I shouldn't have been rescued from the Mawreg," he said.

Immediately she protested but he kissed her into silence. Resting his head on the top of hers, Marcus sighed. "Team guys like me have a Mellurean mind implant for suicide—the checkout code, we call it—we're under orders to use if we're captured."

"Who gives a terrible order like that to loyal warriors?" Her own aura would be nothing but flaming anger on his behalf right now.

"It's ok, it's justified. It's a condition every man and woman agrees to before joining the Teams. We know too much, have too much top secret tech, implants and other things. The enemy can't be allowed to have live...specimens. So I should have died, should have killed myself." He snapped his fingers. "Gone in the blink of an eye. Painless, or so I was assured. Why anyone would care about a flash of pain, in a last ditch situation is beyond me. There was a lot of polite puzzlement when I was rescued but I guess eventually Command and the medicos decided I'd been too traumatized and out of it to use the code or to be a source of information for the Mawreg. And I wasn't exactly sane when I was extracted from the experimentation camp. Rescued fairly soon after my capture so the authorities wrote it off and cleared me to be rehabbed and processed out of the military." He gazed into her eyes and his voice shook ever so slightly. "What if the thing the Mawreg put into my mind was to block the code? The bastards know they can't keep Special Forces soldiers alive long enough to interrogate—what if I was an experiment in preventing our deaths?"

"Then the experiment failed."

"I'm alive, aren't I?" His tone was bleak and she understood he was judging himself harshly.

"But your mind was fighting their efforts. You'd walled off the infestation and were actively fighting it. I came along and added my special power to the battle, my ability to fight the essence of what they'd created on its own terms, but you hadn't given up, no matter what the enemy did to you." She hugged him and stood on tiptoe to kiss him. "You survived and came back to report the problem. We'll report it together, and explain how we defeated it. Valuable information for your Sectors no one else has. You'll see. These Mellureans who created your checkout code will certainly understand what we have to say."

"Maybe there's a way to weaponize what the Mawreg used on me. Turn it on them and drop the stuff on its creators when the slimy fuckers least expect it."

Carialle peeked at his aura, pleased by the mix of pearlescent shades representing hope, mixed with the gleaming silver of resolve and Marcus's constant, indomitable blue flames. "Exactly," she said. "This may be why Thuun placed me where I needed to be, to assist you."

"You're the kind of partner a man dreams of finding." He picked her up and cradled her in his arms as he stepped toward the bed. "I don't know how I got so lucky but I'm planning to spend the rest of my life showing you my appreciation. Whether your god sent you to rescue me or not, you still had to make the decision to get involved." He laid her gently on the bed and lay beside her, smoothing her tousled hair away from her face, frowning in concentration as he untangled two strands knotted into a snarl. "Have I told you lately how much I love you?"

Smiling, she held up the hand with the coruscating colors of the opal ring, waving it in front of his eyes.

"Oh yeah, good job me. Guess I got that right." Marcus pulled her close for a passionate embrace, kissing her as if he'd never let her go.

It was a long time before they made it to the giant hot tub for a second bath.

Marcus hated leaving her alone but he felt strongly he couldn't take her into a law enforcement environment before all the legal ducks were in a row as to her status. While he was waiting outside the hotel for his car, he fidgeted, which was not like him. Rock steady nerves were his hallmark in combat, but today he was fighting the urge to go upstairs and check on her again.

"Nice motor in this baby," said the valet, stepping out of the groundcar, leaving the engine running. "They don't make them like this anymore. We washed it for you, courtesy of the hotel."

He tipped the valet a couple of extra credits for not grimacing at driving his grandfather's beat up old groundcar and then drove himself through the city to the planetary police HQ.

He'd sent Sam a vid message the night before, setting up a time to meet, and his old comrade in arms came to the lobby personally when Marcus's arrival was announced to him.

There was the obligatory back slapping and good humor, and Sam gave him a waiver to carry his personal blaster into the building. The men took the gravlift to one of the top floors, chatting easily about trivialities as Sam escorted Marcus to his office, boasting on the way about the spectacular view of the city he had nowadays. Neither of them would ever discuss sensitive subjects in an open gravlift or hallway. Special Forces operators never forgot the need for operations security even after active duty service days were over.

As soon as the door closed behind them, Sam's genial manner vanished. "Secure environment, safe to talk. I've been turning this planet inside out since you vanished. What the seven hells happened to you? And how are you here now, apparently in perfect health and of sound mind?" He went to the side cabinet. "I think this calls for a drink, morning or not. Hell, it's evening on the other side of the damn planet."

"I like the way you think, always have." Marcus accepted the drink and seated himself at the small table off to the side of the room. "Impressive digs you got here. Nice view. "

"Yeah, comes with the title. So, talk to me."

"Did you get me sent here after I was extracted from the Mawreg experimentation camp?"

Sam nodded. "General Farraven got in touch with me when you were on the military hospital ship because he knew you had no family left, and asked if I'd help out. I checked out a no bullshit rehab facility on the eastern continent with a good rep for handling PTSD cases, personally inspected the place and cleared you to be transferred there from the Star Guard hospital. Then you vanished off the board, man. I started asking questions which upset the guy who heads the Felicia Seven veterans' agency. Bastard tried to tell me you didn't exist." He took a long swallow. "Seven hells, after the action we saw together in the service and how many times you saved my worthless hide, don't anyone try to tell me you don't exist. Especially not a fat, full of himself ground pounder medico."

"Yeah, he's as crooked as they come. And he's hand in glove with another piece of work, a Mrs. Trang."

Sam paused as he lifted his glass. "Name sounds familiar. I think we've been watching her for a while now, trying to make a drug case. She walks just this side of the line, you know?"

"I got caught in a vicious scheme of hers about which I'll be swearing out a report on for you today. I'll be happy to testify when it goes to prosecution. I suspect there are quite a few vets caught in this web because apparently it's our benefits and veterans acres she's after, with kickbacks going to the doctor. There were nine other guys in the facility where I was held prisoner but the other patients were already brain dead from the drugs the ring is using for mind control." Marcus clenched his fists, remembering how reluctantly he'd left comrades behind. "I hated to abandon them but there was nothing I could do."

Sam took a hefty swallow of his drink. "So how did you escape? General Farraven told me—and I reviewed the med reports—you were pretty out of it after what the Mawreg did."

"Pure dumb luck. I had help. A woman who worked at the facility took pity on me and rescued me, at considerable risk to herself. It's actually her I'm here about today because she has troubles going way beyond what I was caught up in."

Leaning back in his chair, Sam raised his eyebrows. "What kind of troubles?"

"Amarotu Combine."

Sam whistled and sat forward, all interest. "That's not good. Of course the crime syndicate's in a world of hurt right now because the SCIA recently did a major takedown, cut off the head of the organization, broke up a lot of the crime clans in various Sectors."

"Yeah, I know. The locals are trying to revive the organization in a reduced form on Felicia Seven. Sent a gang of about fifteen guys up to where I was hiding with her. The creeps were trying to get her back. I was a side issue for them."

"Gramps' cabin?"

"The same," Marcus said. "It's all gone now. We had to blow it up to escape. Don't know how many of the bastards got caught in the explosion and I don't care either."

"Sorry to hear about the cabin—we sure had good times there when we were kids, fishing and whatnot. Where's the lady now?"

"I left her at the hotel. I hate leaving her alone but the Baredjim security staff can probably keep her safe for a couple of hours."

Sam raised his eyebrows. "The high rent district all right."

"She's amazing—a special woman. I've got it bad for her, Sam, even asked her to marry me yesterday."

"Congratulations," Sam said, raising his glass. "You moved at light speed. I knew you would, if you ever met the right girl."

"Yeah, I have no doubts about Carialle whatsoever. She's the real deal but she's got complicated problems. She's got no Sectors ID for one thing—she and a bunch of her people were kidnapped by the Shemdylann from outside our interstellar borders and sold to the Combine four years ago. For another, her handler suffered an accident when he arrived on Felicia Seven with her in tow, and she's afraid of being charged with his death, even though she had nothing to do with it. Carialle has special powers and the mob has used her to help commit crimes. She'll testify against them of course, given immunity, but I figure I'd better get her a high priced lawyer, maybe even from off planet—" Marcus broke off, studying the expression on his old friend's face. "What?"

Sam seated himself behind the desk and called up a file on his AI, swiveling the display to show Marcus. "Your lady resemble her?"

The person in the trideo was similar to Carialle in appearance, with the same green hair and jade skin, wearing a plain gray tunic and pants like one he'd seen in Carialle's closet the night he was in her old apartment.

"Yeah, this women could be her close relative all right. Who is she?"

"This is actually a composite of several women who were recently rescued from the Combine on two different worlds, and who helped with the SCIA takedown as I understand it. You're driving around with one of the most sought after sentients in the Sectors right now. Special orders from the Council of Mellurean Minds *and* Sectors Command—if any of her people are found, both organizations are to be notified and in the meantime, the empath is to be treated with kid gloves, protected at all costs."

Marcus felt relieved to a degree. "What's the protocol? She's not going to be separated from me, I can tell you right now, or shipped off anywhere for interrogation. She and I'll be vanishing where you'll never find us if that's the deal. You know I can make it happen."

"Take it easy, no one's trying to separate you from your lady. It's all legit. I know a couple of the people high up in the SCIA who are working the overall case. Evidently the authorities found records on Devir Six indicating one of the Combine's assets might have been shipped to Felicia Seven right before the SCIA moved in but then the trail went cold." He grinned. "Sort of like your records poofed into thin air after you got transferred here under a medical hold. The Mellureans won't allow the empaths to be treated with anything but utmost respect. We should get you both to a safe house under guard right away and then contact the Agent in Charge." Sam shook his head. "Only you could fall into the biggest criminal case in Sectors' history and come out smelling like a rose. Hey, it's too early to discuss, but I need a guy like you in my organization, if you're looking for work. Not returning to active military duty are you?"

Marcus shook his head. "The last mission downrange was it for me. Besides, now there's Carialle to consider."

"And you're sure she's not…using her powers on you? Trying to get help?" Sam's voice was hesitant.

He didn't even remember leaving his chair but Marcus had his hand fisted in Sam's shirt and he was nose to nose with his old friend, who he'd apparently slammed against the wall. "She'd never do that, it would be a violation of her principles. When she rescued me from Trang's hellhole, she didn't know who I was or what I could do for her. I was a guy in bad trouble and she couldn't stand by and watch me die. Carialle is the genuine article."

Sam had his hands raised. "Easy, no insult intended. I had to ask. With a super empath manipulation's a possibility. You're still on a bit of a hair trigger, aren't you?"

Marcus swallowed hard and released Sam, retreating three steps. "Sorry. I've never been in love before and it makes me crazy not being able to ensure her safety properly myself."

"I get it, believe me." Sam sat behind his desk. "Let me pull together a squad and vehicles and I'll go with you to pick her up."

"I heard what you said about all the high level involvement but respectfully, there are no Mellureans here yet. I want a lawyer for Carialle before we're in police hands and certainly before the SCIA shows up. Who's the best on Felicia Seven right now?"

Sam considered. "Actually, Sandara Glynn is probably who I'd call. She bills an hourly rate high enough to beggar a small planet but she's a bulldog for her clients."

"Georg Glynn's little sister?"

"Little no more, trust me."

"Call her then." Marcus settled into his chair. "See if she'll meet us at the hotel. I'm good for whatever her fee is. Carialle and I have another bargaining chip as well, a set of facts the Mellureans and Command need to know. Maybe the upper echelons already do, considering the deferential way you said her people are to be treated."

Sam tilted his head, interest piqued. "Command? Your lady has a military connection in all this? That's new info on the case."

Marcus shifted in his chair. "Has to do with the Mawreg and the checkout code and I really don't want to discuss it."

Sam whistled. "Yeah, no don't tell me. Don't tell anyone. Keep the details for the right ears."

CHAPTER EIGHT

After Marcus left the hotel room with a final kiss—she had to basically push him out the door—Carialle wandered through the suite, at loose ends. She wasn't interested in any of the entertainment or news streams available on the hotel's channels and she was unable to settle. Just as she'd decided to take a long bath in the elaborate tub, although acknowledging it wouldn't be half as much fun without Marcus, the room's door chimed.

Surprised and a bit wary, she went to the portal and opened the comlink. "Yes?"

"Room service." The voice was cheery.

"There's been a mistake—I didn't order anything."

"No, ma'am, you didn't. But Mr. Valerian put in a special order for you at the front desk as he left. He told the concierge to send you a bouquet of flowers, a cup of tea and this breakfast assortment."

How sweet of Marcus! Carialle keyed open the door and moved to allow the hotel employee to escort the room service robo into the room.

He was followed by another man who closed the door behind him as both drew weapons. "You'll be coming with us," said the first.

She sent a wave of power at them, a strong desire to leave her presence, and backed away, trying to remember where she'd left the blaster. As one of the intruders fumbled with the door in obedience to her sending, the other swore and ran after her, catching her by the hair as she got her fingertips on the weapon. Jerking her head and screaming as several strands of her hair were pulled out by the roots, she fell, twisting and firing the blaster at her assailant as she hit the floor. The shot went wide and he caught her in the stun field of his weapon.

Paralyzed, Carialle lay in a heap, barely able to breathe. He nudged her with his toe before bending to grab the blaster from her loosely clenched hand. "Didn't expect me to be immune to your gift, didja? Edmorad thought of everything," he said with a smirk. "Wait here, like a good girl."

She heard him berating his partner as the pair worked over an alteration to the room service robo. Her mind was going at light speed but she couldn't think of any way to combat the effect of the stunner, much less to alert the hotel or Marcus to her peril. No matter how hard she prayed to Thuun, neither her body nor her gifts responded to her will.

Then the Combine enforcer was standing over her again.

"Get ready for a long nap," he said, shooting her with another blast of energy from the stunner. "Welcome to the Amarotu family reunion."

His mocking laugh was the last thing she heard as she lost consciousness.

While Sam was putting through a call to the lawyer he'd recommended, Marcus received his own call. Concerned it might be Carialle, he answered, only to hear the measured tones of the Baredjim's Executive Manager.

"Mr. Valerian, I'm sorry to have to inform you your companion has apparently been abducted from our premises."

Marcus was stunned and hoped he'd misheard. "What in the seven hells are you taking about? How could she have been kidnapped—what about all your security I paid for?"

He saw Sam's head snap in his direction and he switched the com status to a public setting so his friend could listen in.

"Our deepest apologies, Mr. Valerian, but I'm standing in your suite right now and there are clear signs of violence, including blaster fire scars, and the woman is missing. Our AI detected suspicious activity in this hallway, an unauthorized use of a room service robo, and alerted my staff but unfortunately we arrived too late to be of assistance."

"How long ago?"

"Probably ten minutes. We've been searching the hotel premises and grounds, and the robo was found abandoned in the parking structure. We're accessing the vids now but it appears the surveillance system in the garage may have been tampered with. I believe this was an inside job. The Combine must have had a few of their people embedded as sleeper agents on my staff."

Sam took the com from Marcus's hand. "This is Chief Inspector Garamonte, Felicia Law Enforcement. Preserve all evidence, keep the rooms sealed. I'm sending a squad immediately and I'll be arriving shortly myself."

"Yes, Inspector. Mr. Valerian, we can offer you the assistance of the D'nvannae Brother assigned to this facility."

"We can talk about your offer later." Marcus ended the call and paced across the office, swearing. "I shouldn't have left her. I understood how badly the Combine wanted her after the assault on Gramps' cabin but I figured I had a short window of time to get to you and get help. I figured she was in more immediate danger from the SCIA."

"My team is meeting us downstairs with the groundcars. Let's get to the hotel and see what clues the kidnappers may have left." Sam opened the flap of a closed cabinet, revealing an assortment of weaponry. As he selected a blaster, he said over his shoulder, "I'm making you a special deputy on this case. Plays hell with the regulations but you're probably the girl's best hope. Can you think of any details to provide us a lead? Anything she shared about the Combine on Felicia?"

Marcus shook his head. "She'd just arrived and her handler 's contact failed to show."

As they were about to leave the office, there was a hasty knock and a man burst in, nearly running over Marcus. He looked past Marcus to address Sam. "Sorry, chief, but you said this Combine case was top priority. Combine manager Edmorad Zymmer was observed boarding a private flyer a few minutes ago, after loading cargo into the hold. He's got Gisen Trang and a few other suspicious types with him. The team doing surveillance says it appears he's headed to the compound on Revva Island. We've heard rumors of a big meetup and the island might be the location. Or with Trang along, it could be a big drug deal. Either way, could be the break in the local Combine takedown we've been waiting for."

"Trang. Now there's a nasty piece of work." Marcus shook his head. "Where have I heard the name Edmorad before? Lords of Space, Carialle said he was the person her controller talked to briefly, before he died. He was number four guy in the hierarchy for a while where she used to be based. She's with the bastard, I'm sure of it. Probably inside the cargo container—the Combine makes the empaths travel sealed into crates to avoid detection, according to her." He grabbed Sam's arm. "Forget the hotel—we have to follow this guy if we're going to save her."

"Are you sure? If I concentrate my resources on Edmorad and we've guessed wrong the Combine could ship her offplanet and we'll never find her," Sam said.

"I'm positive. Especially if he has that bitch Trang with him. Send a team to do forensics at the hotel, sure, but we're wasting time. He'll know where Carialle is, if she isn't with him. I've got to get to the island. I'll go by myself if you won't authorize it."

Sam pointed at the officer who'd brought the news. "Assemble a tactical team, full gear. We're going in to take Edmorad and his associates out of play and potentially rescue a highly important witness."

"You got it, chief. Meet you on the roof in ten." The man saluted and hurried into the hall, barking orders into his com.

Sam pulled Marcus in the other direction. "We need to gear up for an assault—body armor, the works. Edmorad's been building an army of enforcers and thugs."

Carialle felt as if she had gritty sand flowing through her veins rather than blood as she struggled to regain consciousness. Attempting to sit up, she realized she was strapped down. Adrenaline making her heart pound, she opened her eyes to discover with horror she was restrained in a padded chair and there was a medical infusion unit attached to her arm, humming as it delivered unknown medication to her system. The room she was in appeared to be an old style library, with wide windows open to the sea, where she heard the waves pounding on the shore. Terrified, she struggled, unable to scream or call for help because she'd been gagged.

"Awake now, are we?" Edmorad Zymmer strolled into the room, holding a glass full of ruby red feelgood, which he sipped appreciatively. "You've led me quite a chase."

She tried to throw a wave of her power at him, but none answered her call.

"I'll bet that expression on your face means you're trying to influence me. Force me to to let you go baack to the boyfriend perhaps? Your special trick won't work right now," he said, wagging a finger. "The medicine we're pumping into you dulls your nervous system quite effectively, until you adapt to it. But by the time you're fully addicted your self-determination will be gone." He snapped his fingers. "You'll be mine, body and soul."

Carialle recoiled in horror as a new person entered the room—Mrs. Trang. The clinic director crossed the floor rapidly and slapped Carialle across the face with angry force. "You've cost me everything, you stupid alien bitch. " She raised her hand for a second blow but Edmorad caught her wrist smoothly, hauling her off balance to face him instead of Carialle.

"Now, now, I don't need my asset damaged. I want her controlled. Obedient."

"Oh she will be, the toranquidol will assure total control over her." Trang jerked herself free of the boss's hold and smoothed her dress, casting a baleful sideways glance at their prisoner. "The human test subjects at the lab on the west side of the island were compliant and coherent until we ended the experiment and terminated them. Most interesting to document the phases of fatal withdrawal. Another vital piece of research."

"She's trying to say we've been making improvements to the original formula, "Edmorad told Carialle, toying with a lock of her hair and yanking her head closer to him when she tried to lean away from his touch. "I've been assured now it'll be possible to completely destroy the subject's free will and maintain them in a steady state with regular doses of the improved toranquidol. You won't descend into the vegetative mode like Mrs. Trang's unfortunate patients did, and I won't have to insist on your wearing a dangerous explosive necklace to keep myself safe. You'll cheerfully do anything I tell you to do."

Carialle shook her head in denial, even as she was terrified Edmorad's threat was valid.

"I'll check on your status in a while—I'm going to have work for you to do tonight as a matter of fact. When my associates are assembled." He tapped his fingers on the medunit hooked to her arm. "This new formula works much more quickly than what Trang gave your boyfriend."

Edmorad turned and beckoned to Trang, chewing one elegant fingernail while glowering at Carialle. "I'm not leaving you alone with my asset. The chem tech can monitor her while we join the others for dinner."

As the two walked out of her field of vision, Carialle dropped her head against the cushioned chair holding her prisoner. A new person strolled into the room, gave her a cursory inspection, fiddling with the controls on the medunit and then moving to the desk. She tried to call her power to influence the chem tech to release her but the man paid no attention, sitting at the huge desk, watching music trideos. She couldn't read his aura. Even if he'd been genetically immune to her power, she'd still be able to see the colors of his soul so the failure told her the medication pumping into her body was suppressing her abilities in terrifying fashion.

She had no doubt Marcus would do everything in his power to find her, but there was no way he'd be in time. Even his ring had been stripped from her finger while she was unconscious. Her thoughts were already fuzzy and disjointed. Without access to her power, she was helpless. Weeping, she closed her eyes and prayed to Thuun to strike her dead before she could be made into a mindless weapon, possibly even deployed against Marcus himself.

Priestess.

The voice in her head was like the rushing wind, deep and swirling with power.

With a jolt, she remembered she was indeed now a priestess, thanks to Marcus, and as such had access to a power denied to those of lesser standing with the god. She didn't need her innate power to influence her enemies to assist her or harm themselves. By the grace of Thuun, she now had the power to cast death itself. It hadn't worked on the completely alien Shemdylann when the enemy dropped from the Tulavarran skies and the priests and priestesses sang the death song. The Combine members in this house were as humanoid as she was, however. And there were no more Tulavarran hostages to be slaughtered in revenge if she disobeyed Combine orders. She wondered how many people were gathered in this location. To her knowledge the death song only worked on a few individuals at most before the spell caster was exhausted.

If the song goes on too long I'll die as well. The dark realization was strangely comforting. She'd rather perish than become a helpless tool for Edmorad or his cronies. At least under the Combine rule before, she'd been able to find ways to rebel, to save a few of the targets, to twist the results she'd been commanded to achieve. There'd be no such wiggle room in the future—from what the Combine manager had said, she wouldn't even care if innocents were hurt. Of course since the Combine had no idea how a gifted Tulavarran replenished his or her power from the energies of the plants and the planets, she might not last long in any case. No one would know to give her access to what she needed and she'd be unable to tell them. The captives had guarded their secret closely. But she'd drunk deeply from the old growth forest surrounding the cabin. Her reserves at the moment were substantial.

Overthinking. With a start she realized her mind was going in circles while the toranquidol dripped ruthlessly into her body. *Wasting precious time.*

But one had to sing to cast the death spell and she was gagged.

Carialle made strangling sounds against the gag, tossing her head and convulsing in the restraints, banging the medunit on her arm against the chair with a loud crash.

The chem tech left his chair and stepped to her side. "Now what?" he said. Checking the medunit, he muttered snatches of tech talk about absorption rates and blood oxygen levels while Carialle did her best to feign dying by strangulation. "Oh fuck it," the man said eventually as he unfastened the gag and threw it on the floor, kicking it under the chair. "I'm not listening to this fuss you're making for the next hour."

She drew deep breaths.

"You're not actually in danger of choking," the tech said. "You're getting plenty of air. But I don't want to be annoyed by all the freaky behavior and racket. Can't hear my own music vids. Now be a good girl, get over your anxiety attack, sit and take your meds. You act up again and I'll not only put the gag back, I'll make you wish you hadn't bothered me twice." He walked to the desk and resumed watching the miniature trideos.

Quietly, under her breath, Carialle hummed the death song to herself, pulling the power into her core and preparing to cast it. The tech's loud music covered up her own efforts and she was able to concentrate sufficiently to hold to her song, not be influenced by what he was listening to. Regret and sorrow at never seeing Marcus again twined through her preparations and firmly she pushed them away. *Let my dying thought be of him, of our love.* The fatal energy roiled in her being, hungry to strike at her enemies, who were also the enemies of Thuun. Opening her mouth, she sang at full power. The tech was the only person she could see. He startled from his chair as she sang the first notes, hands over his ears, staggering toward her, but collapsed within a few feet, writhing in agony.

Dimly, Carialle heard screams in the distance as she continued to sing, emptying herself of every bit of stored energy, determined to kill this nest of snakes even as she died.

Chapter Nine

"No activity on the island, sir," reported the tech seated at the scanner board as the police flyer sped through the sky in formation with two others, all heavily armed. "No one's scanning us, no signs of life."

"You're sure Edmorad was on his way here?" Marcus asked, gripping his pulse rifle. His gut told him there wasn't any margin of error for finding Carialle. A wild comet chase to the wrong Combine location could mean he'd lose her forever, and he wasn't prepared to accept that. Half formed plans for demanding help from the Mellureans were in the back of his mind, if Carialle wasn't here.

"Our surveillance team tailed him here, then stood down, away from the island, holding station, as per orders," the lieutenant in charge said. "We're coming in on the complex from the island's blindside."

Marcus studied the landscape below, composed mostly of gigantic *baytim* trees, reaching for the sky, balancing on platforms of roots burrowing through the salty ocean waters and into the soil below. A few outbuildings came into view to the starboard.

"Seeing motionless targets on the ground now, sir, looks like bodies."

Sam and Marcus crowded behind the tech to watch the scanners as the flyer formation swooped closer to the ocean. One man was floating face down in the water next to a boat, and two more lay onshore, weapons close at hand.

"Take us inland and land next to the building complex," Sam said. "I think we're too late for whatever happened."

"A rival Combine faction doing a massive hit maybe?" Marcus asked. *And Carialle a prisoner in the midst of the carnage.*

"Could be. Word on the streets was Edmorad was going to force an alliance of all the surviving units on Felicia this weekend, and put them under blood oath to accept him as overlord. Maybe another Combine manager had other ideas about who was in charge."

The flyer set down smoothly on a pad in the center of the island, close to a large, rambling house with many outbuldings. The other two police craft were landing as Marcus and the cops in his vehicle deployed behind Sam, weapons hot, ready to do battle with any Combine personnel who offered resistance.

But there was none. A few more men lay dead near the landing pad and at the entrance to the house. The medic knelt next to one, checking for a pulse. He shook his head. "Gone, sir. Whatever these people died of was painful, judging from the victim's face and contorted body position."

"Poison gas maybe?" asked a police lieutenant.

"No signs of any toxins," the tech reported, watching the readouts on his scanner. "Could have dispersed in the open air by now."

"Could your lady do this?" Sam asked.

"Maybe. She's got amazing powers." Marcus was wild with impatience to get into the house and search for Carialle. Corpses didn't interest him.

With no further delay, Sam gave the order to move out. The door to the house stood wide open, a woman sprawled dead on the patio.

Marcus paused in his rapid advance, swearing as he caught a good look at her contorted face. "Trang, the bitch who held me prisoner."

"Guess we won't be prosecuting her, then," Sam said. "Pity."

Stepping past Trang's corpse, fearful of what the woman might have done to Carialle, Marcus entered the house, cautiously checking to the right, where he found a dining room in a massive state of disarray, chairs toppled and bodies scattered everywhere. One of the dying had clutched the tablecloth as she fell and lay buried under a pile of dishes and congealing food. Red wine spread on the table linens and the floor like blood.

Sam and his team were right on his six, not waiting for the clear signal.

"Spread out, search for Edmorad," Sam said. "We need to know if there's any chance he escaped. Preserve any evidence."

Marcus fidgeted. Carialle was clearly not in this room and not being a cop, he didn't care about evidence or crime scenes. He was driven by the belief time was ticking away for the woman he loved. "I'm going to do a sweep of the rest of the house."

"I've got your six," Sam said, leaving the table where he'd been examining an open, active AI. "Lieutenant, take charge here. You two, come with us."

Marcus prowled down the hall, checking the other rooms along the way with a rapid once over before signaling clear and moving on. At the end of the house was a massive library and there he found Carialle, strapped to a chair, another dead man on the floor. "Seven hells!" Stowing his weapon on his back, he ran forward, clawing at the humming medunit to turn it off and get it away from her. She lolled in the chair like a doll with no stuffing, head to the side, blood dripping from her ears. Huge violet shadows lay under her closed eyes and she looked as if she too had succumbed to whatever magic she'd unleashed. "Carialle, angel, wake up." He slashed the restraints on her wrists and ankles with his knife and caught her as she fell forward. A soft breath stirred his hair as he checked her neck for a pulse. "Weak, intermittent. She's alive but barely." His own heart stuttered at finding her alive.

"Medic!" Sam's shout was peremptory. He jerked a thumb at one of the men with them. "Go get him. This kidnap victim is our top priority."

Tenderly Marcus lifted Carialle from the chair and took her to a couch along the wide wall, laying her on the plush cushions before kneeling at her side. Leaning close, he kissed her cheek, which was icy cold under his lips. "Stay with me, angel, help is here." Her eyelids flickered but she didn't open her eyes or respond in any other fashion. He rubbed her arms and laid his hand tenderly against her cheek where a huge green and purple bruise spread in an ugly circle. "What the hell did those bastards do to her?"

"Apparently she got her revenge on them, whatever they had in mind." Sam bent over and picked a container off the desk near the couch "Toranquidol," he read from the label.

"The drug Trang used on me at the clinic," Marcus said, "But it didn't work this fast."

The medic arrived and shouldered Marcus aside to take Carialle's vitals. "Not sure what we can do for her, sir," he reported to Sam over his shoulder. "She doesn't register on the instruments as anything we've seen in the Sectors before so the AI has nothing to recommend as treatment. Don't have an antidote for that street drug either. Her heart's barely beating. Other organs shutting down. I'm afraid we're going to lose her before we can fly her to the mainland, sir."

Marcus stood by her head, resting one hand on her shoulder so she'd have peripheral awareness he was there for her. The medic's grim words hit him like so many heavy stones. *This is impossible— I'm not going to let her die.* But he was no doctor, had no magic like she did, what could he do?

The medic rummaged in his kit, debating with himself out loud between two courses of medication. "Not sure if she can tolerate either of these and the drug used on her is highly resistant to the effect of stimulating agents."

"Adrenaphix worked for me," Marcus said.

A dubious expression on his face, the medic shook his head. "Not sure her system could take the jolt from an upper that strong right now."

"Do your best," Sam said. "Every minute we keep her with us is a chance we can get her real help, at a hospital or maybe from the Mellureans. I put out a call on the case before we left."

Marcus shook his head. Sam's words were so much static to him, with no real hope for Carialle. She needed an intervention now to save her life. He clenched his fists and bowed his head, furious he had nothing to offer her.

Warrior.

The voice in Marcus's head was like a torrential downpour of rain or a huge wave crashing on the shore. He staggered, hand to his forehead, dizzied by the power flowing in the wake of the single word.

He shoved the medic out of the way and bent to lift Carialle into his arms. "I know what to do."

The cops were uncertain, upset at the way he'd treated their comrade. They didn't know him the way their boss did and moved as if to interfere with his leaving the room.

Juggling Carialle, he pulled his pulse rifle up to menace the men between him and the door.

Eyes narrowed, jaw set, Sam evaluated him for a moment, before making a 'back off' gesture to his men. "Let him pass. He's got a plan and you heard the medic tell me there's nothing we can do."

Marcus ran out of the house, Carialle's body featherlight in his arms. He thought she curled into his embrace but couldn't be positive. He sprinted toward the shoreline, where there was a beach of white sand, bracketed by centuries' old stands of the baytim trees. Selecting one towering fifty feet above the others, he headed toward it. Sam was running with him, stride for stride.

"I'm getting up on the platform of roots and then I need you to hand her up to me," he said to his old friend as he ran holding Carialle close to him.

"Anything you say."

He and Sam stopped at the base of the tangled roots and Marcus allowed Sam to take Carialle for the few moments he needed to use vines to climb to the low platform where the actual trunk of the massive tree began, resting on a bed of hundreds of interwoven root tentacles. He reached for Carialle, getting a good grip under her arms as Sam lifted her and raising her to join him. Her head bobbled and he was afraid to check her pulse now. Watching his step as a bright green serpent hissed and slithered away, he crossed the uneven surface. Gently Marcus laid her beside the tree and knelt beside her. He took one of her hands, spreading the fingers wide with his own and pressed it against the smooth surface of the trunk, holding her hand in place with his.

"Come on, angel, I can't do it for you," he said. "This tree has to be old enough for what you need." Bending over, he kissed her cheek. "Please, Carialle, fight for your life, for our life together. Come back to me."

There was no response, not even a flicker of her eyelids.

"I'm your warrior but I can't do my job without you at my side. Remember the colors? Our hearts entwined? I'd die for you, angel, if it would help."

Her fingers twitched in his and her skin tone was healthier, with a bit of warmth to his touch. Closing his eyes he tried to visualize the swirls of color she'd shown him, the ones she said were their bond. But he dealt in realities, not psychic visions, which gave him an idea. "Her ring is missing," he said to Sam without taking his focus away from Carialle. "See if your men can find it?"

He heard Sam murmuring into the com and then his friend raised his voice. "Buddy, I'll support you all the way here, but what's supposed to be happening?"

Marcus shook his head, unwilling to explain Carialle's secret, reluctant to even breathe the truth of what he was attempting because to speak the words aloud would reveal how foolish his hopes were. Surely if Carialle needed to replenish her psychic energies to live, the process should be organic, right? Automatic? *What if she needs to say special words to kick it off?* Well, he couldn't do anything about that. He released her hand for a moment and set aside his weapon, then gathered her firmly into his arms and again placed her hand on the tree, with his protectively over it.

He closed his eyes, trying to put himself back into the battle they'd waged for his life—was it just four days ago? Toward the end of the fateful night he'd felt as if he was floating between life and death and only Carialle's fierce energy had kept him anchored, to this world and to her. He needed to do the same for her now. Leaning over, making sure to keep her palm on the tree, Marcus kissed her. "I'm here," he whispered. "I'll do whatever you need me to do, just stay with me."

A touch on his shoulder. "My men found her ring, in Edmorad's pocket," Sam said. "I've got it here. Your grandmother's ring, the heirloom from old Earth?"

"Yeah, thanks." Marcus accepted the piece of jewelry and slid it onto the ring finger of her left hand as Sam stepped away. "Our pledge to each other, remember?" he said softly into her ear.

The colors of the strange gem in the center of the setting gleamed in the waning afternoon sunlight and Marcus focused on the kaleidoscopic show. No matter how he moved the ring, the red hue predominated and he remembered how she'd said it was the color of their love. Keeping their contact with the tree intact, he hugged her close, blinking away an unexpected burning in his eyes. "Seven hells, Valerian, suck it up." Now was *not* the time for unaccustomed weakness over the fear of losing her—she needed his strength. "Please," he said, not sure to whom he was speaking—his own Lords of Space, her Thuun, someone, no one.

Carialle stirred in his embrace. Her lips parted and he leaned close to hear the single word. "Both."

What in the seven hells does she mean? Hoping he was guessing correctly, he pressed her left hand to the smooth trunk of the tree as well, startled by a flash of red light from the opal. Blinking, he realized his hands were growing uncomfortably warm, as hers heated where they rested on the bark.

He heard birdsong overhead and risked a glance upward into the dense foliage to see a multicolored flock had arrived and settled onto the branches, all their focus on Carialle and him. The birds were singing softly.

Song.

Song was always a key for her.

The birds were trying to help her.

Marcus cleared his throat. He was no singer, although he'd been told he had a good baritone voice. Rejecting a momentary embarrassed reluctance because of Sam lingering close by, he opened his mouth and launched into a song he remembered his mother singing to him as a child, repeating the same refrain over and over. Then he segued into another, realizing a moment too late it was a bawdy drinking song from his Academy days, but he could and did put a lot of energy into it.

Finishing the tune, he took a breath, evaluating Carialle's condition, encouraged to see the shadows under her eyes fading.

He did a doubletake, the song faltering as he leaned in to take a better look. Tiny purple flowers were blooming in her hair. Surely the blossoms had to be a good sign? His heart pounded and he sent another incoherent prayer to the Lords of Space.

Her eyelids flickered and slowly she opened them, staring up at him with those great emerald and golden eyes that had so captivated him from the moment he first met her. "Marcus?"

"Here, always." He wanted to crush her to him but was afraid to disrupt her link with the tree, so he settled for a kiss he gentled even as he began the caress.

"Were you singing?" Her voice was thready.

"I'd do anything for you, even sing. The birds gave me the idea."

"How did you know what to do to help me? To bring me to the tree?"

He remembered the uncanny rush of a voice in his head and shrugged. "I can't explain—maybe because I love you?" He stroked one of the strands of her soft green hair, admiring the petite velvet petalled blossoms. "Did you know you have flowers blooming on your head?"

"Really?" She struggled to sit upright and removed her hand from the tree to grab a section of her hair and see for herself. "These are *violamikri*, the flower of true love. I believed them to be a legend because supposedly the blooms only appear when a priestess experiences true love for one of Thuun's warriors."

"Well that's how I feel about you too, even if I can't grow fancy flowers on my skull to prove the point." He kissed her with more emphasis now, tasting her, pulling the sweetness of her life force into himself through their connection, relieved she was going to survive. "They'd be pretty silly on my head." He was so happy he didn't care if he was making corny jokes.

"Where are we?" She craned her head.

"On the island the Combine brought you to, but don't worry. I'm here with the cops. The danger's over. You took care of the situation yourself, didn't you?"

"I knew you'd come for me—I never for a moment doubted you—but Erdoman and Trang were going to make me a mindless slave with the toranquidol so I had no choice but to sing the death song. Forgive me?" Tears trickled down her cheeks.

He hugged her and wiped away the tears with his fingers. "You did what you had to do. I understand."

Staring fixedly at the patterns in the tree bark, she asked, "The Combine members are all dead?"

"Every fu—every bad guy on the entire island. I'm in awe of your power. Of course you nearly killed yourself too and it'll take me a while to get over the fright."

"I'd rather die by my own power than risk being enslaved by the Combine again." Her voice was hard.

"I think you're a warrior and you did what you had to do," he said again, sensing she needed reassurance.

"I need to communicate with the sentient embodied by this tree," she said a bit apologetically. "And reach through it to pull from the planet's energies to be fully healed. May I have a few moments alone? I can't concentrate with you so close, not after being terrified I'd never see you again. You're distracting in the best possible meaning of the word." Her smile warmed him all the way to his toes.

"I'll take that as a compliment. Count on me to follow up on it later, when you're more yourself." He squeezed her free hand. "You do whatever you need to do and I'll wait at the edge of the tree's root platform, over there. I need to check in with Sam anyway—he's probably going nuts wanting to know what's happening. Promise you'll tell me if you feel weak or sick again."

"Of course." She caught his hand as he rose. "But not too far away?"

"No more than a few feet, I promise. I'll be right over there."

Marcus walked to the edge of the root platform, where Sam waited. He heard a low murmur behind him as Carialle chanted to the tree.

"Situation stabilized?" Sam asked.

"She's doing fine, maybe a bit shaky. We'll be ready to move out soon. I don't think she'll want to stay on this island a moment longer than she has to."

He checked the beach below where armed cops with weapons hot stood in a ring around their baytrim tree. "What's with the defensive cordon?"

"I got a reply already from the SCIA and the Mellureans—both parties are sending reps to Felicia Seven to interview your lady. And you. I've got strict orders to take good care of you both." Sam dug his AI out of his pocket. "You should find this reassuring—the Mellureans pushed through a Sectors ID for Carialle, making her one of their affiliates, under their protection. No one's going to touch her if it means messing with them."

Impressed but on the alert for any threat to his lady, Marcus scanned the message and shrugged. "All good but I still want our hotshot lawyer to meet us as soon as we reach the mainland and a safe house."

Sam stuck the AI in his utilities' pocket. "No problem. I get it—you and I saw too much bureaucratic bullshit during our time in the Teams. Better to be safe than sorry."

"Exactly, although I tend to trust the Mellureans. Not that those tight lipped, all powerful sentients give us much choice in the matter." Marcus checked on Carialle for a moment, relieved to see her on her feet, one hand tracing a knothole in the tree trunk. "Looks like she's wrapping up her convo with the plant. We can go soon."

Sam raised his eyebrows. "She talks to trees? For real?"

"It's a long story, tell you over a beer sometime."

As he predicted, Carialle joined him shortly, putting her hand into his.

"Angel, meet Sam Garamonte," Marcus said, gesturing at his friend. "Sam, this is Carialle, my fiancée."

"Pleased to meet you. I didn't think Marcus here would ever settle down. Quite a player, this guy—" Grunting as Marcus elbowed him sharply in the ribs, Sam shut up and shook hands with her. "If you're ready, I've got a flyer standing by to take us to a safe house on the mainland."

She shuddered. "Please get me away from this place."

"You're going with us? What about all the evidence to be gathered at the crime scene?" Marcus asked his friend.

"My orders are to stick with you like a binary star in your orbit," Sam said with a laugh. "I'm guessing it'll be very interesting, with the company you're going to be keeping, hobnobbing with the Mellureans and all. I've got a good investigative team and my staff won't miss any significant forensics, whether I'm here to supervise or not."

Sam left the root platform and then he and Marcus helped Carialle descend to the beach as a police flyer landed nearby. Sam sprinted ahead to confer with his men, and Marcus and Carialle strolled hand in hand behind him, surrounded by their bodyguards, who expanded the perimeter and gave the couple ample room after Marcus glared at them.

"Will I be in trouble for what I did here?" she asked in a low voice. "Will you be in trouble?"

He squeezed her hand. "We'll both be fine. I've got a lawyer on tap and Sectors authorities are excited to talk to us. I think we're probably in for a few weeks of testifying—you more than me obviously but I'll be right there the whole time."

"Making plans for our escape if we don't like the experience?" she asked with a smile.

"Count on it, angel. No more barefoot middle of the night sorties either."

"Could we get married now?"

"Would you like that?"

Studying her ring in the sunlight on the beach, she nodded.

"We'll get it done right away then. Sam can make the arrangements. I'll put him to work once we're in the flyer. He's a good guy, one of the best, and he was the person searching for me here on Felicia Seven."

"He would have rescued you if I hadn't," she said.

"Not in time." Marcus was adamant. He stopped and turned her to face him, unable to resist taking a kiss. "I think you and I were meant to be, and nothing can change the facts. I needed you—I'll always need you."

"Hey, lovebirds, the Sectors are waiting," Sam yelled from the flyer's ramp.

"He offered me a job, by the way," Marcus said as they strolled forward. "As a cop, working with him."

"A fitting occupation for a warrior," she said.

"You won't mind? Or be worried?" Marcus was surprised at her calm demeanor.

"You have the blue flames of Thuun," she reminded him. "It's your purpose in life to protect and fight for what's right. I'll have to find meaningful work I can do here since the Sectors have no need for a priestess to petition my deity. There must be useful employment for a woman who can nurture living things."

Squeezing her hand, he said, "We'll figure it out together, after the honeymoon."

"Could we go back to the cabin eventually? I know it was destroyed, which will be painful for you to see, but it was in such a lovely spot. I long to return there." She tapped her chest, over her heart. "The place calls to me powerfully. I know we could find much happiness there."

"I was thinking we could rebuild the place," he said, "If you cared to set foot in the forest again."

"Considering the happiest moments of my life occurred there, with you, there's nowhere else I'd rather be. And the setting is so beautiful, full of ancient trees and bountiful lifeforce. I realize there'll be destruction and debris but the forest can grow over the wounds. There was much I longed to explore but we had no time."

"I'll be establishing better defenses when we rebuild," he said with a laugh. "If you thought Gramps was intense, wait till I upgrade with new tech. No one will be intruding on our privacy again."

"We'll have to live in the city most of the time though, won't we? If you're on the police force?" Her expression and dubious tone of voice made it clear she wasn't happy at the prospect.

"There are better districts than River Wind. And we'll make sure to buy a place with a big garden. I still have my veteran's acres allotment, thanks to you, remember?"

"I think we can build a good life." Carialle paused to stare at the ocean waves for a moment. "And besides, maybe Thuun has further need of a warrior and a priestess."

"Like sending us on a quest? Now you're scaring me. Or you would be, if I was afraid of anything other than losing you. Which I'll take good care never to allow." He laughed as he swept her into his arms, to carry her into the flyer as Sam led the way. "Did you pause to consider the possibility maybe he brought us together expressly to save each other? Mission accomplished, debt to Thuun paid, we can live happily ever after."

"I think he has more for us to do," she replied. "But the prospect is exciting— we'd both grow bored in a life without suitable challenges. Admit it."

"I won't argue but I'd like a nice long honeymoon first." Marcus carried her through the flyer's hatch and placed her onto the seat Sam indicated, taking his place beside her. "Put in the request next time you're talking to Thuun, priestess, would you? Oh, and he should give us time to do adequate planning, as long as we're making a list of our must-haves for any new adventure."

He shifted his attention to Sam momentarily, as his friend relayed news about the upcoming meeting with the lawyer and the move to the safe house. Carialle gazed out the flyer's window, watching as the island fell behind them, growing smaller until there was only the expanse of the sparkling sea underneath her. A feeling of peace spread throughout her, body and soul.

Marcus squeezed her hand to draw her attention from the view. "Are you hungry? Thirsty? Need anything at all?"

She kissed him. "Just you, for the rest of my life."

***

Thank you for reading TWO AGAINST THE STARS! I really hope you enjoyed the adventure (and of course I'd love a review if you have time and the inclination to write one – even a few sentences would be wonderful. Authors relish reader feedback).

- If you'd like to stay up to date on all my new releases, please sign up for my newsletter at http://wordpress.us7.list-manage1.com/subscribe?u=2a 337b96e2ee1ee1250004b9d&id=7462393c9e.
- STAR CRUISE: STOWAWAY and DANGER IN THE STARS, the books which tell the stories of two other Tulavarran prisoners, and how they escaped from the Combine, are available at ebook retailers now so be sure to look for those if you haven't read them

ALSO BY VERONICA SCOTT

Science Fiction Romance

Wreck of the Nebula Dream

Star Cruise: Marooned

Star Cruise: Outbreak

Star Cruise A Novella: Stowaway Plus Rescue and Golden Token

Short Stories

Escape From Zulaire

Mission to Mahjundar

Hostage to the Stars

Trapped on Talonque

Star Survivor

Danger in the Stars

Lady of the Star Wind

Ancient Egyptian Romance

(with a dash of the paranormal too!)

The Gods of Egypt Series

Priestess of the Nile

Warrior of the Nile

Dancer of the Nile

Magic of the Nile

Ghost of the Nile

Healer of the Nile

<u>Fantasy Romance</u>

The Captive Shifter

ABOUT
VERONICA SCOTT

Best Selling Science Fiction, Fantasy & Paranormal Romance author, as well as the "SciFi Encounters" columnist for the USA Today Happy Ever After blog, Veronica Scott grew up in a house with a library as its heart. Dad loved science fiction, Mom loved ancient history and Veronica thought there needed to be more romance in everything. When she ran out of books to read, she started writing her own stories.

Seven time winner of the SFR Galaxy Award, as well as a National Excellence in Romance Fiction Award, Veronica is also the proud recipient of a NASA Exceptional Service Medal relating to her former day job, not her romances! She recently was honored to read the part of Star Trek Crew Member in the audiobook production of Harlan Ellison's "The City On the Edge of Forever."

Blog: https://veronicascott.wordpress.com/
Twitter: https://twitter.com/vscottheauthor
Facebook: https://www.facebook.com/pages/
Veronica-Scott/177217415659637?ref=hl